Camp Club Girls

Bailey's
ESTES PARK EXCITEMENT

Edited by Jeanette Littleton.

ISBN 978-1-60260-295-3

Scripture taken from the HOLY BIBLE, NEW INTERNATIONAL VERSION®. NIV®. Copyright © 1973, 1978, 1984 by International Bible Society. Used by permission of Zondervan. All rights reserved.

This book is a work of fiction. Names, characters, places, and incidents are either products of the author's imagination or used fictitiously. Any similarity to actual people, organizations, and/or events is purely coincidental.

Cover design: Thinkpen Design

Published by Barbour Publishing, Inc., P.O. Box 719, Uhrichsville, Ohio 44683, www.barbourbooks.com

Our mission is to publish and distribute inspirational products offering exceptional value and biblical encouragement to the masses.

Printed in the United States of America.
Dickinson Press, Inc.; Grand Rapids, MI 49512; October 2010; D10002531

Camp Club Girls

Bailey's
ESTES PARK EXCITEMENT

Linda McQuinn Carlblom

BARBOUR
PUBLISHING

CHAPTER 1

Two Mysteries, Five Days!

Crsiiish!

The ground shook.

Bailey Chang grabbed her father's arm.

"Does Colorado have earthquakes?" she shouted over the sudden noise.

"Stampede!" someone yelled.

Bailey's dad grabbed her. With his other hand he snatched her friend Kate Oliver. He dragged them to the safety of the Stanley Hotel's front porch. Bailey's mom and older sister, Trina, ran up the steps.

A herd of beautiful elk thundered across the lawn of the old hotel. Within seconds, only a cloud of dust and an unnatural silence remained.

Moments earlier Bailey's greatest fear was of the historic Stanley Hotel itself. Nestled in the majestic Rocky Mountains in Estes Park, Colorado, it had stared menacingly at Bailey, each window a glaring eye, as her family drove up and parked. Its deathly white walls and blood-red tile roof eerily reminded her of the ghosts rumored to live in it. The bright sun hid behind clouds on this early October afternoon.

Bailey swallowed hard, her dark brown almond eyes wide. In her nine years, she had never stayed in a haunted hotel. Nor had she almost been trampled by a stampeding herd of elk.

"Is everyone okay?" Mr. Chang asked as the dust settled.

"I think so," Mrs. Chang answered. "Are you girls all right?"

"Except for being almost killed in a stampede, we're great!" fourteen-year-old Trina mouthed off.

"A—Are we really going to stay here?" Bailey asked her father, George Chang, who had brought the family along on a business trip.

"Yes," he answered matter-of-factly. "It's a well-known hotel, highly recommended. I'm sure that stampede was merely a fluke."

Bailey looked at her eleven-year-old friend, Kate Oliver. Kate's eyes were as big as twin full moons behind her black, rectangular glasses. She nervously tucked her sandy, shoulder-length hair behind her ears. Biscuit the Wonder Dog whined and hid behind Kate's leg. Bailey, Kate, and the other four Camp Club Girls had rescued Biscuit when they first met at Camp Discovery. Though Biscuit lived with Kate, he still took part in some of the girls' mysteries.

"But what if it's true, Dad?" Bailey asked.

"What if what's true?"

"What if there really are ghosts in there?" Bailey

pointed at the hotel.

"Bailey." Mrs. Chang's hands rested firmly on her hips, her blond head tilted. "Do you really think your father would let you stay in a dangerous place?"

"Think about it, Bales," Trina said, relaxing now that the threat had passed. "Mom and Dad barely let us go to sleepovers without interrogating our friends' parents first. They're pretty picky about where we sleep."

Bailey's shoulders slumped slightly. "I guess you're right."

Kate looked over a pamphlet for the hotel that she'd picked up at the Denver, Colorado, airport. "Maybe we can study this brochure about the hotel and investigate the ghost sightings and mysterious sounds people have reported."

She grinned at Bailey and grabbed Biscuit. "And Biscuit the Wonder Dog will sniff out clues for us." Biscuit's whole body wriggled and wagged as he licked Kate's face.

With the stampede over, Bailey's family returned to unloading their Honda CR-V in front of the hotel. "Come on. Let's go get checked in," Mr. Chang said, starting toward the main entrance.

The huge front porch seemed friendly enough, Bailey thought, now that she didn't need to escape from rampaging elk. Cushioned white wicker rocking chairs, love seats, and tables sat waiting for people to relax in their comfort. *Maybe it won't be so bad.* Bailey took a deep breath and stepped through the doorway.

Bailey smelled old wood and lemon oil as she entered the magnificent lobby, pulling her pink camouflage suitcase. Gleaming hardwood floors reflected her awestruck face. She was so busy looking around that she nearly ran into an enormous flower bouquet on a round, glass-topped table.

A wide, grand staircase with a white banister and glossy-wood handrail invited—or dared—guests to go upstairs and explore ghostly nooks and crannies. On each end of the lobby overstuffed couches and chairs rested on large area rugs in front of fireplaces. An old green car with yellow wooden wheels in mint condition stood on display near one of the fireplaces, protected by thick red velvet ropes.

"That car's called the Stanley Steamer," Kate explained to Bailey. "Here's a picture of it in this brochure. The guy who started this hotel, F. O. Stanley, invented it. See, there's his picture."

The girls surveyed antique black-and-white portraits of F. O. Stanley on gray-green wallpapered walls.

"Wow," Bailey said. "This looks like where a movie star would stay."

"I've never stayed in a place this fancy before." Kate shoved her glasses up her small, roundish nose. "Sure beats the Super Six where we usually stay."

"Sure does." Mrs. Chang turned a slow circle to take it all in. "I'm glad George's company is paying for this."

Bailey parked her suitcase and joined her dad, who was

standing at the registration desk. Her mom, Trina, and Kate followed close behind.

"Usually the elk are quite friendly as they roam about the town," the clerk with a name badge that said "Barbara" was saying. "But for some reason they've become aggressive in the last few weeks, so be cautious around them."

"What made them become so aggressive?" Bailey asked, standing on tiptoe to see over the counter.

The registrar shrugged her shoulders. "One minute they're calm and the next thing you know, they're charging. No one knows why."

"That's unusual." Kate scratched her head. "There must be a reason for their sudden change."

"Don't worry," Mrs. Chang said, putting one protective arm around Bailey's shoulder while patting Kate's back with the other. "We'll be careful. Right, girls?"

The two nodded but smiled at each another. Biscuit yawned and whined at the same time.

Barbara leaned over the counter. "Is that your dog?"

"He's mine." Kate smiled proudly then picked up the wiggly fur ball. "This is Biscuit." The dog's whole body wagged in a friendly Biscuit greeting.

Barbara frowned. "Is he house-trained?"

"Of course!" Kate answered.

"Does he bark?"

Bailey almost blurted out, "Not as much as you!" but Kate answered coolly, "Only when threatened."

9

Mr. Chang quickly stepped in. "I'm sure Biscuit will be no trouble. We'll make sure he stays quiet and doesn't make a mess. And if he does, we'll take full responsibility for any extra cleaning charges."

"Just make sure you keep him on a leash." Barbara gave the Changs their keys and a map of the hotel, and then she called a bellhop to take the suitcases to room 412. "The elevator is right over there or you can take these stairs," she instructed the Changs, pointing to her left.

"Let's ride the elevator," Kate suggested after hooking a leash to Biscuit's collar.

"After walking through the airports, I'll be glad to take the easy way to our room." Mrs. Chang smiled. "I can't wait to get out of these shoes!"

The five climbed into the elevator and Bailey pushed the button for the fourth floor. A ding signaled their arrival. The doors opened to a long hallway with plush burgundy carpet.

"Look at that wallpaper," Bailey said in awe. The lower portion of the wall was painted white, and the upper was papered with a white-on-white embossed design. Bailey touched it. "It's not wall*paper*—it's wall *fabric*!"

"Whoa!" Kate reached out to feel it, too, before following the arrow directing them to room 412.

As the girls walked down the hall, two boys who looked about their ages came out of one of the rooms. Lunging, Biscuit growled and barked at them.

Kate yanked him back with the leash. "Biscuit!" She picked up the little dog and looked at the boys. "Sorry."

One of the boys shrugged while the other gave her a fiery glare.

"I hope that isn't any indication of how this week will be." Mr. Chang stopped outside of room 412. He slid his magnetic card through the slot and pushed the door open.

Bailey walked in and eyed the sparsely furnished room. "Cool! It looks so old-fashioned!" Two full-size beds with tall posts at each corner stood against one wall. A wooden table and chair sat in another corner. Bailey looked around. "Look how high these beds are! They even have little steps to help you get into them!"

A rollaway bed was pushed along one wall, ready to open.

"Let me guess," Trina said. "That's my bed."

"You girls can trade off if you want." Mrs. Chang looked softly at her older daughter.

"That's okay. At least I won't have to sleep with anyone."

"I'll let you use our stairs if you want help getting into your rollaway," Bailey offered.

Trina laughed. "I think I can get into this bed without steps. But thanks."

"No way!" Kate shouted. "Come see this bathroom!"

Bailey hustled to the door and peered in. A claw-foot bathtub sat next to the toilet. A freestanding toilet paper holder and a pedestal sink completed the décor.

"I can't wait to take a bath in that tub," Bailey said. "It's just like in the old movies. I'll need lots of bubbles."

Back in the bedroom, Mrs. Chang put her suitcase on the bed and began to unpack. "Dad and I will take this bed and you can have the one by the window," she said to Bailey and Kate.

"I have a meeting this afternoon, but you can get settled while I'm gone," Mr. Chang said. "I should be back before supper."

"Okay. See ya later, Dad." Bailey hugged her dad's neck. "Don't get run over by any wild elk!" she joked.

Kate climbed onto the bed by the window. "Let's look at this brochure to see what we can find out about this place."

"Yeah, maybe we'll learn where the ghosts hang out." Bailey shuddered, then grinned. She sprawled out on the bed beside Kate.

"Let's see." Kate laid out the brochure before her like a map. "This tells the history of the hotel, and about F. O. Stanley, inventor of the Stanley Steamer automobile, who came to Estes Park for health reasons. He and his wife spent a summer here in 1903 and fell in love with the area. Because of his health improvement and the beauty of the valley they decided to stay and opened the Stanley Hotel in 1909."

"Interesting," Bailey remarked.

"Sorta, but listen. . ." Kate's eyes sparkled. "The hotel was the inspiration for a novel by Stephen King. It's also been used as a location for a bunch of films."

"Cool! We're actually staying where they made movies!" Bailey exclaimed. "Maybe we'll see some stars. Or *maybe* some of their stardom will rub off on *me!*"

"You don't need anything to rub off on you to become a star," Mrs. Chang said. "You're special in your own right. But remember, you need to finish your education before you run off to Hollywood."

Bailey laughed and sat up. "But wouldn't it be awesome? To be a famous actress making big movies?"

Trina rolled her eyes as she hung one of her sweaters in the closet. "You've dreamed that dream for s–o–o–o long."

Bailey glared at her sister. "So what?"

"So you have to do something besides sit around and dream about it, that's what." Trina poked her younger sister in the ribs. Bailey rolled to her side, giggling.

Biscuit jumped onto the bed to check out the commotion then nested comfortably against Bailey's back.

"All right. Now, where were we?" Kate asked, looking at the brochure. "Oh yeah! I was just getting to the part about the ghosts!"

"Oooooo!" Bailey gave her best ghost shriek, making Biscuit howl.

Kate laughed as she scooped the little dog into her arms. "Don't worry, boy. Ghosts aren't real."

"What's it say?"

Kate pushed up her glasses. "It says F. O. Stanley's ghost is the most notable one seen. It usually appears in the lobby or the Billiard Room, which was his favorite room when he was alive. His wife, Flora, has been seen playing the piano in the Music Room. Cleaning crews also have heard strange noises coming from room 418, as well as finding the bed rumpled when the room has been empty. And guests say they hear children playing in the halls at night. One guest saw a man wearing a cowboy hat and a mustache staring out of the window of room 408 when no one was in the room."

"Since even numbers are on one side of the hall and odd on the other, that makes room 408 only two doors down from ours!" Bailey exclaimed. "Do you think we'll see any of the ghosts?"

Kate answered in her scariest voice, "You never know," then laughed evilly.

"Stop it! You'll scare Biscuit." Bailey petted the dog.

"Biscuit?" Trina glanced sideways at her sister. "You sure he's the only one you're worried about Kate scaring?"

"Well, I'm not scared of any fake ghosts, if that's what you mean." Bailey crossed her arms defiantly and lifted her chin.

Trina smirked. "Right."

Kate pushed her glasses up. "Since ghosts aren't real, these sightings and sounds must be done by some special effects." Bailey could see the wheels turning in Kate's head. "Maybe we can uncover how they do them."

"Yeah!" Bailey agreed. "Another Camp Club Girls mystery! Does the brochure say anything else that might help us figure it out?"

"Not much. Just that room 401 is usually the ghost hunters' favorite room." Kate put the pamphlet on the nightstand.

"Hey, check this out," Trina called, pulling back the curtains.

Bailey and Kate jumped up from the bed.

"Awesome!" Bailey pressed her nose to the window. Below their fourth floor window was a grassy courtyard where elk wandered among the guests as if they'd checked in and paid for a room themselves.

"They don't seem aggressive," Kate said.

"Maybe not now, but you can't be too careful around wild animals," Mrs. Chang warned.

"I wonder what they eat," Bailey said. "Maybe we could get some elk food and feed them."

"No way." Mrs. Chang shook her head in no uncertain terms. "You heard what the lady at the desk said. They can become aggressive without warning. Wildlife can be very unpredictable."

Trina moved away from the window and went back to unpacking her suitcase. "I wonder what makes them get angry and charge people."

"Maybe they're afraid the people will hurt them," suggested Bailey.

"Or maybe someone did hurt them and it has made them skittish," Kate offered.

"Maybe they've got some hideous sickness like mad elk disease and it will gradually infect the whole elk population!" Bailey grimaced.

Trina laughed. "You two have a lot of crazy ideas. Maybe they're just sick of tourists like us invading their town."

"Looks like we'll have two mysteries to work on while we're here." Bailey held up one finger. "One, what makes the ghosts and spooky sounds, and two, what made the elk turn mean."

Bailey looked at Kate, two fingers still raised like a peace sign. A grin spread slowly across her face. Kate beamed back then raised her hand and Bailey high-fived it. The Camp Club Girls had two mysteries and only five days to solve them.

Ghost Hunt

"Mom, can Kate and I go explore the hotel?"

Placing clothes into the dresser drawers, Bailey's mother answered, "I suppose. But take the hotel map with you and your cell phone, just in case you get turned around."

"Okay, thanks!" Bailey turned toward the door.

"And don't forget Biscuit," Trina added with a smile.

"We would never forget you!" Kate cooed in a baby voice to her dog.

"And stay together," Mrs. Chang warned.

"We will," Kate promised.

"You still have the brochure about the hotel?" Bailey asked her friend.

"Right here." Kate patted her back pocket before hooking Biscuit's leash to his collar. "Let's go, boy."

"Don't let any ghosts sneak up on you!" Trina called as they left.

Bailey laughed. "That shouldn't be a problem since ghosts don't exist!"

"Let's find room 401 while we're on this floor," Kate

suggested as the door closed behind them. "Since it's the ghost hunters' favorite room, maybe we'll see something that will explain how they do some of the special effects."

"Good idea." Bailey looked both ways down the hall. "Our room number is 412, and I think the numbers were smaller nearer the elevator, so let's go that way."

"Even-numbered rooms are on our side, and odd on the other."

Bailey studied the oval plates outside each door that showed the room numbers. "Here it is," she whispered when she spotted room 401.

"Why are we whispering?" Kate asked.

Bailey laughed. "I don't know. I feel like I'm spying or something."

Kate examined the walls and then inspected the carpet. "I don't see anything suspicious. Do you?"

Bailey shook her head as she inspected the hallway. "There's a speaker, but that's where the music is coming from. Nothing weird about that."

"We'll have to keep our eyes and ears open," Kate said, still searching. "I'm sure this isn't that complicated if we just keep thinking."

Trying to peer underneath the door, Bailey ventured, "The tricks could be hidden inside the room." She stood back up. "I can't see anything. Maybe we'll have better luck at room 217, the room where they say the author of that scary book stayed."

"It's worth a try," Kate said.

The girls found an elevator and stepped inside.

"Did you read that book or see the movie that was made from it?" Bailey asked as the doors closed.

"No, it's a horror movie. My parents won't let me watch scary movies like that. Did you see it?"

"Nope." Bailey grinned mischievously. "I think our parents are just alike. Mine would never let me see scary movies, either."

"Hey, I wonder if Elizabeth saw it." The elevator bell dinged as the doors opened onto the second floor. Kate stepped out first with Biscuit in tow. "She's fourteen. Maybe her parents let her watch those kind of movies."

Bailey flipped open her cell phone and pushed *E* in her contacts. Elizabeth's number showed up and Bailey pushed TALK. Kate spotted a sign that pointed to room 217 and they followed its arrow.

"Elizabeth? It's Bailey."

"And Kate!" Kate shouted into the phone.

"Well, this is a surprise!" Elizabeth said. "What are you two up to? Are you really together or are we conferenced in?"

"We're together," Bailey said, and went on to explain where they were and why. "And guess what? We've already got two mysteries to solve!"

"Two?" Elizabeth asked.

"Yeah, the elk here have gone bonkers," Bailey explained. "I think they might need a counselor or something!"

Elizabeth laughed. "Maybe we should have them talk to McKenzie. She's good at figuring people out, maybe she could help the elk, too!"

"Maybe! So that's our first mystery." Bailey's voice rose with excitement. "Our second one is hunting ghosts. People say ghosts live in this hotel. But since we know ghosts aren't real, we're trying to figure out who is making them seem real, and what special effects they use."

"Wow! Sounds exciting!" Elizabeth paused a moment. "So how can I help? You know I love a good mystery."

Bailey told her that a book by Stephen King was inspired by the hotel, and that a movie had been made from the book. "Have you ever seen it?" Bailey looked expectantly at Kate.

"If it's a Stephen King movie, I haven't seen it," Elizabeth answered. "My folks won't let me. Too scary." She added, "And I'm glad."

Bailey laughed and then shook her head at Kate to relay Elizabeth's answer. "Yeah, I know what you mean. I don't really want to see those scary movies, either. We just thought since you're older you might have seen it."

"Let me talk!" Kate grabbed the phone. "Hi, Elizabeth! Biscuit says hi, too."

The girls chatted for a minute and then Elizabeth said, "Well, you know I'm praying for you two! Keep me posted on what you find out."

"We appreciate your prayers," Kate said. "We'll let you

know what we find out and if you can help out on anything else. If you talk to any of the others, let them know we'll be calling or e-mailing them soon with all the mystery details."

Kate flipped the phone closed just as they came to the end of the hall.

A metal room plate by the door read 217.

"Here we are! Just think. Movie stars stood at this very place we're standing." Bailey nearly felt faint from the rush.

"And just think," Kate repeated just as dreamily. "A future movie star is standing here right now!"

"Oh, stop." Bailey waved her hand. "You're just saying that."

"You never know. It could happen." Kate dug in her pocket and brought out a pen. "Here. Let me take your picture, just in case. Then we can say I predicted your fame on this very day at this very moment outside this very door!"

"Hold it! That's not a camera. It's a pen." Bailey shook her head.

"Ah, you *think* it's a pen, but it's really a tiny camera!" Kate smiled brightly. "I've been dying for the right moment to show you my latest gadget!"

"Let me see that." Bailey took the pen from Kate. She clicked the top of it, and the ballpoint came down just like a real pen. She scribbled on the corner of the brochure. Blue ink looped round and round. "So it's a real pen *and* a camera. How does it work?"

"You look into the silver clip to see what the camera sees. Then click the top and it takes the picture."

"Did I take a picture when I clicked it before?" Bailey asked.

Kate shook her head. "It only functions as a camera when it's held on its side. Up and down, it's just your ordinary, average blue pen. Turn it over and it switches to camera mode."

"That's awesome!" Bailey squealed. "Let's try it. Take my picture." She struck her most glamorous pose.

Kate held the pen on its side and clicked the top.

"How do we see the picture?"

"We have to unscrew the pen and remove the memory chip inside. I have a special stick to put it into that will fit the computer, then we download the pictures."

"I can't wait to see how it turns out." Bailey bounced up and down on her toes.

"Me, too." Kate looked around. "Let's see if we can find any clues here."

A door burst open down the hall and a man bolted out. "Oh no! We've got to go help them!" he shouted to the woman behind him.

"I hope no one was hurt!" she cried as she and the man ran past the girls.

Bailey looked at Kate and they took off after the man and woman, who had stopped in front of the elevator. The elevator doors opened just as the girls caught up and they all climbed inside.

"What's going on?" Bailey asked.

"We were looking out our window when we saw an elk run through the courtyard knocking a boy to the ground," the man answered. "We're going to see if he needs help."

"My husband is a doctor," the woman explained.

Bailey nodded somberly, and Kate petted Biscuit.

The elevator door opened into the main lobby. The doctor and his wife rushed to the courtyard where the elk had charged.

Bailey and Kate stood a short distance away but stayed close enough to see and hear what was going on. In the courtyard, a boy who looked about six years old was stretched on the ground. He didn't appear to be injured, but his father was kneeling over him. The doctor hurried to them.

"Sir, I'm Doctor Gibbins," the man said, kneeling by the father. "I saw what happened from my room and came immediately in case the boy was injured. Is he your son?"

"Yes," the father answered. "Thank you."

The boy moaned and turned his head.

"Did the elk step on him or just knock him down?" asked Doctor Gibbins.

"He was knocked down and bumped his head."

The little boy tried to sit up.

"Hold on there, son." The doctor gently checked his arms and legs to make sure no bones were broken.

"Daddy!"

"I'm right here, Robby," his father answered tenderly.

"I think he's going to be fine," the doctor told him.

"Seems to have gotten the wind knocked out of him and a good bump on his head when he went down, but nothing too serious." He helped the child sit up.

"Thank you," the father said again, clasping the doctor's hand.

Robby's dad stood up and picked up his son. "Let's go see Mommy."

From the sidelines, Bailey looked at Kate. "Wow! That was scary."

"Guess what they said about the elk was true." Kate stuffed her pen back in her pocket.

"Did you have that out the whole time?" Bailey asked.

Kate nodded. "I took a few shots just in case it turned into a major news story or something." She laughed. "They might need some pictures for the evening news."

Bailey rolled her eyes. "You're always thinking."

"It'll be a good test to see how well the pictures turn out since we were farther away."

"I wonder what made the elk run like that?" Bailey eyed the courtyard.

"Something must have set him off."

The two girls strolled through the courtyard looking for any clue of what might have spooked the elk but found nothing.

"This really is a mystery." Bailey sighed. "A mystery with no clues."

"There's bound to be something we're missing," Kate

encouraged. "We'll figure it out."

"Come on. Let's head back to the room."

⏤•⏤

That night, while Mr. Chang and Trina went to get ice, and Mrs. Chang read a book, the girls reviewed their day.

"After looking around here a bit I think we're starting to learn our way around, don't you?" asked Bailey.

"Yeah, the map in the brochure was helpful," Kate replied. Then wrinkles lined her forehead. "I felt bad about that little boy getting hurt by the elk."

"I know. Me, too," Bailey said.

"I'm glad he seemed to be all right."

"That camera-pen of yours is awesome!" Bailey grinned like she'd just won a prize at the fair. "I can't wait to see the pictures you took today."

The hotel room door opened and Mr. Chang and Trina walked in with a full ice bucket. "Anyone want some ice for a bedtime drink of water?"

"Yeah!" Bailey ran into the bathroom to grab the plastic-wrapped glasses. They scooped ice into each one and added water from the tap. "Thanks!"

"Are we ready for lights-out?" Mr. Chang asked.

"Just a minute," Kate replied. "Let me spread Biscuit's blanket at the foot of the bed." She and Bailey laid out the paw-printed fleece blanket, and Biscuit turned a tight, complete circle before plopping down on it. "All set!"

Mr. Chang flipped off the light. "Good night."

"'Night, Dad." Bailey lay in the dark with her eyes open. Moments later, she heard soft giggling.

"Girls, get to sleep." Mrs. Chang used her no-nonsense voice.

"We're *trying* to," Bailey answered, confused.

The giggling came again, this time followed by childlike voices.

"Bailey, you heard your mother," Mr. Chang warned sternly.

"Dad, it isn't us!" Bailey complained.

"Then who is it?" Trina smarted off.

"How should I know?"

The voices came again, the words unclear, but sure.

"It's the ghost children in the hallway!" Bailey yelled, sitting straight up.

Ghost Children of the Night

Biscuit gave a low, throaty growl.

"Ghost children?" Mrs. Chang said, getting up. "Really, Bailey, I think you've been reading too many mysteries."

Bailey switched on the bedside lamp. "Hand me that hotel brochure, Kate." She pointed to Kate's suitcase, where she could see the brochure sticking out.

Again they heard faint laughing and children's voices.

"Did it ever occur to you that those could be real children out there, rather than 'ghost children,' as you call them?" Trina leaned on one elbow in her bed.

"Listen to this," Bailey said, folding the pamphlet back. "Guests often say they hear children playing in the hallway at night. One couple even checked out of the hotel very early in the morning complaining that the children in the hallway kept them up all night. However, there were no children booked in the hotel at the time. The children have since been called 'ghost children of the night.'" Bailey lowered the hotel brochure and nodded emphatically. "See? Ghost children."

"I seem to recall seeing some boys in this hallway when we brought our luggage to our room," Mr. Chang said. "Two boys. We could be hearing them, or any other children who are checked in."

"If we hear the voices again, can I peek out the door to see if anyone's out there?" Bailey asked.

"If you promise to get right to sleep afterward," Mr. Chang answered with a yawn.

"Me, too?" Kate asked.

"You, too."

"Yeah, that way there'll be a witness when the body snatchers grab Bailey," Trina teased.

"Trina!" Mrs. Chang scolded. "That will be enough from you. Can we all just relax and get to sleep?" She flipped the light off.

Hee-hee-heeeeee!

"That's them!" Bailey said, jumping into her slippers and bathrobe. "I'm out of here!"

Trina groaned. Biscuit barked fiercely then bounded off the bed and ran to the door.

"Me, too!" Kate felt her way through the dark after Bailey.

Cautiously, Bailey slid the security chain off the door and slowly opened it. Light from the hallway spread into the room in a giant wedge. She poked her head out into the hall and looked from side to side. "I don't see anyone."

"No surprise there," Kate said, joining her in the doorway.

28

"Mom, can we go down the hall?" Bailey whisper-yelled.

"Just grab the key off the table first. And stay in our hall," Mrs. Chang instructed in a tired mumble. "I don't want you wandering the entire hotel in your pajamas."

Bailey felt her cell phone on the table and opened it, shining its light to find the key. "Got it," she told her mom. "We'll be back in just a minute."

"Stay, Biscuit," Kate commanded. "We'll be right back."

With the phone lighting their path, the girls crept back to the door and stepped into the lighted hallway. Bailey shoved her phone into her bathrobe pocket. A high-pitched giggle greeted them, followed by muffled children's voices that sounded like they were telling secrets.

"There it is again!" Kate's eyes scanned the walls then moved up and down from floor to ceiling as if looking for some clue as to where the voices came from.

"Sounds like they're coming from down here," Bailey whispered loudly, walking to the far end of the hall. The voices spoke again, though still not clearly.

"There must be wires to a speaker somewhere," Kate said. She ran her hand along the wall, stopping at the corner. "Here!"

Bailey hustled over to her friend.

"Feel right here," Kate instructed.

Bailey touched the wallpaper on one wall then continued around the corner. "Aha! A bump!" She ran her hand vertically along the bump and found that it went higher than she could reach. "Our wire!"

"Now we just have to figure out where it runs to and we may have our first solution to the ghost sounds." Kate's eyes sparkled like diamonds, and she gave Bailey a victorious high five.

"Come on," Bailey said. "We'd better go back so my mom doesn't worry."

The two tiptoed back to the room. Bailey lit her cell phone up again once they arrived in the dark room and led the way to their bed. Biscuit jumped at their legs, excited to see them as if they'd been gone for months. Kate and Bailey pulled back the sheets and climbed in, followed by Biscuit, who snuggled into his little nest of blankets on the bed.

"We'll have to investigate some more tomorrow," Kate whispered.

"Should be a great way to start the day!" Bailey smiled and then drifted off to sleep.

•—•—•

The next morning, Bailey woke to the sound of the phone and her father's voice. She rolled over and pulled her pillow over her head.

"Yes, I'll be available in an hour. Thank you. See you then."

Mr. Chang flipped his cell phone closed and said to Mrs. Chang, "William Perkins will meet me in the hotel lobby in an hour for our conference. His wife and children are here with him, and he's bringing them to meet us. They're also staying at this hotel."

"Guess I'd better clean up." Mrs. Chang sprang from the bed and headed to the shower.

"Will has two boys, so I don't imagine the girls will be too interested in hanging out with them much."

"Or will they?" Mrs. Chang said with a sly smile. She laughed and shook her head. "Probably not, but it will be nice to meet them anyway. It's always nice to have a friendly face, just in case you need something." Mrs. Chang turned on the water. "Will you get the girls up while I shower?"

Mr. Chang moved to the girls' bed and whispered, "Biscuit!" The dog stretched and yawned, but soon he was prancing all over Bailey and Kate, nudging Bailey's pillow off her head, licking hands, faces, and feet.

"Biscuit! Stop!" Kate howled, hiding her face in the covers.

"We're too tired. Go away." Bailey rolled over.

"Come on, girls," Mr. Chang said. "Time to get up. Some people are meeting us downstairs in an hour."

"Ugghh," Bailey moaned.

"You, too, Trina." Mr. Chang shook his older daughter's shoulder. "Mr. Perkins is bringing his family to meet us."

"How could you do this to me?" Trina wailed, with all the dismay she could muster at seven a.m.

"Easy!" Mr. Chang chuckled. "Watching you writhe around and moan is good early morning entertainment."

Trina threw a pillow at her father, which he deftly dodged. When she saw him pick up the pillow and pull his arm back to throw it, she jumped up. The pillow landed with a *whoosh* in her empty bed.

"Ha!" Trina laughed. "Missed me!"

"Ha, yourself." Mr. Chang laughed. "I got you up."

Bailey and Kate had pillows in hand ready to throw but put them back down when the action wound down so quickly. "Shucks," Bailey said. "We missed our chance."

An hour later, they stepped out of the elevator into the hotel lobby.

The Perkins family was looking at the old Stanley Steamer car in the lobby when the Changs arrived.

"Will! Great to see you." Mr. Chang and Will Perkins shook hands.

"George, I'd like you to meet my wife, Janice, and my sons, Joseph and Justin."

Bailey inhaled sharply and elbowed Kate. Joseph and Justin were the two boys Biscuit had nearly attacked in the hall the day before. Good thing they'd taken Biscuit for an early morning walk and left him in the room before coming to meet the Perkinses.

"It's a pleasure to meet you," Mr. Chang replied, shaking each of their hands. "This is my wife, Dory, and my two daughters, Trina and Bailey. And this is Bailey's friend, Kate."

Bailey smiled politely.

"Hey, aren't you the ones who had that dog in the hallway yesterday?" Justin asked.

Mr. Chang cleared his throat. "I guess we are. I'm sorry,

I didn't recognize you. We're terribly sorry about Biscuit barking at you. He's a little skittish being in a new place and off his usual routine."

"No harm done," Mr. Perkins assured him.

Bailey noticed that Justin, the older of the two, was scowling. *What's his problem?*

Her thoughts were interrupted by a friendly looking older man and his wife approaching them. "There they are!" the man said.

"Grandpa!" Joe ran to the couple, who greeted the boy with warm hugs.

"Hungry for some breakfast?" Grandpa asked him.

"Starving!"

Mr. Perkins introduced his parents, Glen and Clara Perkins, to the Changs.

"They live here in Estes Park. That's why I brought the family along," Mr. Perkins explained.

"We're off to have breakfast at the Waffle House," Grandma Perkins said. "You're welcome to join us."

"George and I need to get to our conference," Mr. Perkins said. "But maybe Dory and the girls would like to."

"That would be lovely," Mrs. Chang said before Bailey could signal that she did not want to eat with these grouchy boys. She turned her back to the group and rolled her eyes at Kate.

After getting directions to the Waffle House, Mrs. Chang, Trina, Bailey, and Kate piled into the car. "That was

nice of them to invite us to join them for breakfast," Mrs.
Chang said.

"Nice if you like eating with Oscar the Grouch," Bailey
retorted.

"Bailey!" her mother warned.

Bailey looked down at her lap. "But Mom, those boys
are so rude!"

"Maybe they're not morning people," Mrs. Chang said.

"Apparently they're not afternoon people either, since
they were so grouchy yesterday when Biscuit barked at
them."

"Maybe they're afraid of dogs," Trina said.

"Who could be afraid of sweet little Biscuit?" Kate asked.

"As I recall, Biscuit wasn't exactly his usual, sweet little
self when he barked at the boys." Mrs. Chang turned into
the Waffle House driveway. "Let's just give them a chance.
We don't know what's going on in their lives. Maybe they're
having some kind of problems at home or something."

Bailey nodded. She never thought of that.

"Right this way." The hostess grabbed menus and
motioned for them to follow her to two tables pushed
together.

Bailey sat next to Kate, with Justin and Joe directly
across from them. While the adults chatted pleasantly, the
children were silent. Bailey cleared her throat. "So how old
are you?"

The dark-haired boys shifted in their seats. They

seemed uncomfortable making conversation with the girls.

"I'm twelve," Justin said, eyes narrowed.

"And I'm ten," Joe added less than enthusiastically.

"You're about our ages, then," Kate volunteered. "I'm eleven and Bailey's nine."

"What about her?" Justin nodded in Trina's direction.

"That's Trina. She's fourteen."

"Umph," Joe said.

Whatever that means, thought Bailey. She eyed the boys more closely. They weren't bad looking. They could even be considered cute if they smiled more. Freckles sprinkled Joe's nose and round cheeks. Justin's face was more chiseled and his build was more muscular than his younger brother's. His eyes burned with anger or hurt or something Bailey couldn't quite identify. His eyebrows pointed downward in what looked like a permanent frown.

"Did you hear about the elk problem they're having?" Kate asked, trying to be polite.

"Of course we did," Joe snapped. "Our grandparents live here."

"Oh, right," Bailey said. She added, "Did we say something wrong?"

"What do you mean?" Justin placed his hands on the table, palms down as if he were about to jump up.

Bailey shrugged. "Well, you just seem mad at us."

"Why should we like you?" Joe scowled.

"Why shouldn't you?" Kate smiled in spite of herself.

35

"We don't have anything against you. We just don't like your dog." Justin leaned back and folded his arms.

"Have you had a bad experience with dogs before?" Bailey asked.

Joe watched his older brother, waiting for his answer. "Maybe, maybe not."

"Well, I'm sorry if you did," Kate said. "Biscuit is a really nice dog, and he'd never hurt a flea."

"Whatever." Justin picked up his menu and hid behind it.

"Have you eaten here before?" Bailey asked, changing the subject.

"Our grandparents bring us here all the time," Joe said, suddenly sounding almost friendly.

"What do you recommend?" Kate asked.

"I usually get the Belgian waffles with strawberries and whipped cream." Joe licked his lips.

"What about you, Justin?" Bailey asked.

"I don't have a favorite," he said from behind his menu.

"I'm thinking of the ham and cheese omelet," Kate said. "Ever had it?"

Justin lowered his menu slowly. Bailey saw his jaw clench. "I've had it and it's fine," he said through gritted teeth.

Were those tears in his eyes? Bailey blinked to see more clearly. Too late. The menu was back up again.

The waitress took their orders and they ate their breakfast without much conversation.

Afterward, Mrs. Chang and Trina went to do some

shopping while Bailey and Kate took Biscuit for a walk and talked about their strange encounter with the Perkins boys.

"Something was definitely bothering Justin," Kate said.

"No kidding!" Bailey's eyes nearly popped out of her head. "Did you see when you asked him if he'd had the omelet before? I thought he was going to cry!"

"We need to get on our Camp Club Girls Web site to let the other girls know what's going on around here. So far we have elk gone mad, unexplained ghost noises, and two crabby boys who hate us for no reason." Kate stopped to let Biscuit sniff some bushes.

"Maybe Justin and Joe don't hate us, but they sure do act weird," Bailey said.

Back at their room, Bailey opened her laptop and signed onto the CCG Web site then clicked on the chat room. Kate pulled out her cell phone and also went to the site.

> Bailey: *Hi CCGs. Who's out there?*
> Elizabeth: *I'm here.*
> McKenzie: *Me, too.*
> Sydney: *Me three!*
> Alex: *Me four!*
> Bailey: *Perfect! Kate and I are in Estes Park and have some weird stuff we may need your help with. We're staying at the Stanley Hotel, which is supposedly haunted. We've heard some strange noises and voices and are trying*

to find out what causes them.

McKenzie: *Oooo! Sounds spooky!*

Elizabeth: *How can we help?*

Bailey: *We heard the ghost children of the night in our hall last night.*

Kate: *I found a wire running along the wall under the wallpaper. It probably goes to a speaker somewhere. It was higher than I could reach, so I lost track of it.*

Alex: *Sounds just like a* Scooby Doo *episode! They always have fake ghosts. Maybe you'll run into Shaggy and Scooby while you're there!*

Bailey: *Any hints you can give us?*

Alex: *I think you're on the right track with the speaker wire. You just have to find the speaker.*

Kate: *I figure it's probably a recording. Something probably trips a circuit to start it. But what would be tripping the recording to play?*

Alex: *Look for a switch of some kind. It will most likely be hidden. Something people would touch unknowingly. Or at least that's how they did it in Scooby.*

Kate: *Great. We'll look around some more.*

Bailey: *We also are trying to find out why the elk (which roam around town just like people!) are suddenly going crazy and are charging for no reason.*

Kate told Bailey, "Tell them about Justin and Joe."

> Bailey: *Kate wants me to tell you about these two boys we met.*
> Alex: *Oooo! Sounds interesting!*

Kate rolled her eyes at Bailey. Leave it to Alex to get the wrong idea about boys.

> Bailey: *It's not like that. These boys are crabby. Even Biscuit doesn't like them.*
> *We're not sure what's up with them, but we hope to find out.*
> Kate: *Bailey has already nicknamed the older one Oscar the Grouch.*
> Alex: *And the younger one?*
> Bailey: *I'm thinking of Slimey, you know, like Oscar's worm friend on* Sesame Street.
> McKenzie: *LOL. Maybe they're insecure and trying to make up for it by being tough.*
> Bailey: *Maybe. We don't know too much about them yet except their dad works with my dad and their grandparents live here in Estes Park.*
> Elizabeth: *Do you know much about elk? What would spook them?*
> Bailey: *We haven't researched elk yet. Any volunteers?*

Sydney: *I can check them out. My Uncle Jerome lives in a cabin on South Twin Lake near the Nicolet National Forest in Wisconsin and has elk around his property.*

Bailey: *Great. Thanks. If anyone reads anything about special effects that could be used to make ghost sounds, let us know. We'll keep you posted on any new developments. Bye!*

Bailey closed the laptop and sighed. "I wish we could all be together to work on our mysteries."

"It's great that we can at least stay in touch so easy, though." Kate suddenly sat up straight. "Hey! We never finished exploring the wire we found under the wallpaper last night."

"Let's go!" Bailey was off the bed faster than you could say "ghost children of the night."

"You stay here, Biscuit," Kate said. "We won't be long."

Kate brought along her camera-pen, and Bailey her camera-watch. There were no ghost noises in the bright sunlight of afternoon. A neighboring door opened and Justin and Joe came out, binoculars hanging around Justin's neck. They stopped short when they saw Bailey and Kate.

"Hi, Justin. Hi, Joe," Bailey said. "Where you going?"

"Hiking." Justin kept his eyes to the floor.

"That sounds like fun," Kate said. "Maybe we can go with you sometime."

"Yeah, maybe," Joe answered, his eyes meeting Bailey's.

"We don't know our way around the trails like you probably do since your grandparents are from here," Bailey said, trying to build the boys up just in case McKenzie's idea about them being insecure had any truth to it.

"Hmmph," Justin grunted. He pushed past them.

"What's that long thing under your jacket?" Bailey asked.

"Huh? Oh this?" Justin looked flustered and pulled his jacket closed even more. "It's just my walking stick."

Bailey and Kate nodded as the brothers dashed to the elevator.

The girls turned to each other.

"That was no walking stick," Kate said. "It was way too short."

"And it looked like it was made of metal." Bailey frowned.

"Bailey!" Kate's eyes were wide with alarm. "I think you're right! That metal walking stick was really the end of a long gun!"

The Angry Elk

When the elevator doors closed behind Justin and Joe, Bailey and Kate went to a hallway window to see if they could spot the brothers leaving the hotel. They were about to give up when the boys came into view and walked across a grassy field into a wooded area.

"Where do you think they're going?" Bailey asked.

"And why do they need that gun?" Kate added.

Bailey turned from the window and started back down the hall. "Those two are up to no good."

Kate followed then stopped. "Bailey, look!" She pointed to a high corner where the hall had a sudden small turn.

Bailey's eyes followed Kate's finger to a flat circle with tiny holes in it. "A speaker!"

"Exactly!" Kate ran her hand along the wall. "Aha!"

"Aha what?" Bailey asked.

"What do you wanna bet our wire ends there? I can see a bump under the wallpaper up higher than I can reach, but then it snakes over from the corner to the speaker."

"They probably put it there figuring no one would look

up since the hall jogs to the left here. People would have to watch where they're going so they don't run into the wall."

"Perfect reasoning!" Kate high-fived Bailey. "I mean, look how they wallpapered the edges of the speaker so you barely even see it. A definite attempt to hide it."

"If we hear those ghost children again tonight, let's see if the voices are coming from this speaker."

The elevator dinged, and Mrs. Chang and Trina stepped out, arms loaded with shopping bags. "Oh, Bailey! I thought you and Kate were taking Biscuit for a walk."

"We already did," Kate said. "Now we're investigating the ghost children's voices we heard last night. We think we may have figured it out!"

Bailey wound her hand through the crook of her mom's arm and pulled her toward the corner speaker. "See that flat, round thing up there?"

"Yeah," Mrs. Chang said, craning her neck.

"It's a speaker," Bailey whispered.

"No!" Mrs. Chang responded dramatically.

Bailey giggled. "Yes!"

"Does that mean you won't be spirited away after all?" Disappointment dripped from Trina's voice.

Bailey glared at her.

"Anyway," she continued, turning back to her mom, "if we hear the voices again, can we come down here to see if that's where they're coming from?"

"I suppose," Mrs. Chang answered. "But right now I

have to go put these packages down. They're about to break my arm!" Mrs. Chang and Trina wrestled their bags to the room.

"Wait a minute," Bailey said to Kate. "We know where the speaker is, but how does it come on? Like, is it on a timer or does it have a motion sensor that sets it off? What trips it to play the sounds?"

"We'll have to look for a hidden switch like Alex said." Kate scratched her head. "That will be our next step."

Kate pulled out her camera-pen and snapped a few pictures of the speaker.

"Now that Mom and Trina are back, let's go see what they're going to do this afternoon," Bailey suggested. "Maybe they would take us into town to do some sightseeing." Bailey raised her eyebrows at Kate.

"That would be fun," Kate agreed. "We haven't had a chance to see the town of Estes Park yet."

"Let's go ask," Bailey said, already hurrying down the hall.

●—●—●

An hour later, Mrs. Chang pulled into a parking place outside a row of shops and Trina, Bailey, and Kate, with Biscuit in tow, climbed out of the car. A gentle breeze blew Bailey's hair in her face. She shaded her eyes from the bright sun.

"Did you see those banners hanging over the street?" Bailey asked.

Trina looked around. "Which ones?"

"One said the Elkfest starts tomorrow, and another one said something about a film festival!"

"Elkfest?" Trina looked at her sister like she had sprouted antlers.

"I don't know what it is, but that's what the sign said." Bailey pulled out her cotton candy lip balm and generously applied it.

"I read about that on the Web before we left for our trip," Kate said. "It's a celebration of the elk that live here. There are classes, bugling contests, elk tours, entertainment, and all kinds of activities."

"Bugling contests?" Bailey asked.

"That's the sound the elk make," Kate informed her. "I guess the contest is to see which person can sound most like a real elk."

"Now that would be fun to see!" Trina said, laughing. "Maybe we could get Dad to enter."

"I seriously doubt that." Mrs. Chang smiled. "But it would be funny."

"Can we go, Mom?" Bailey pleaded.

"We can pick up some information about it," Mrs. Chang said. "If it works out, I suppose we could."

"Cool." Bailey started down the sidewalk with Kate and Biscuit, while Mrs. Chang and Trina trailed behind. They looked in shop windows, exploring the stores that interested them. Elk and bighorn sheep leisurely roamed the streets, not nearly as hurried as the humans around them.

"Be careful around those animals!" Mrs. Chang yelled ahead to them. "No fast moves that might spook them."

"Okay," Bailey answered, her eyes glued to the window displays.

"Here's a rock store!" Bailey squealed. "Maybe I can find a good one to add to my collection."

Inside, Bailey buried her hands in the barrels of polished stones, letting them trickle through her fingers, cool and slick. She inspected row upon row of shelves that held rocks and gift items. Impressive displays of quartz, geodes, and turquoise glittered from every aisle. Jewelry cases boasted the authenticity of the gems.

"Wo–o–ow!" Bailey said, taking it all in. "This must be heaven!"

"If you can't find something for your rock collection here, you never will," Kate said.

Bailey gasped. "Look at this!" She held a shimmering rock in her hand. "Gold!"

"That can't be real gold," Kate said. "They wouldn't have it in an old barrel."

"But it looks just like gold," Bailey said. "Even the sign says it's gold."

"Yeah, fool's gold," Trina said from nearby.

Bailey whirled around to face her. "Gold is gold."

"And a fool is a fool," Trina muttered.

"Girls," Mrs. Chang warned.

"Bailey, check out this poster." Kate stood by a large

wooden pillar on which a poster had been stapled. "Estes
Park Film Festival, a weekend of stars."

"Stars? Here?" Bailey's knees nearly buckled.

"That's what it says," Kate replied.

"We've got to keep our eyes open!" Bailey exclaimed.
"This could be my big break!"

"Or heartbreak," Trina mumbled.

"I've got to look my best at all times, just in case!" Bailey
looked down at her sweatshirt and jeans with holes in the
knees. "This will never do!" Her voice rose ever higher,
approaching the panic level.

"Deep breath, Bailey, deep breath," Kate coached her.
She picked up a brochure from a rack of tourist information
and fanned her friend. "Do you need your inhaler?"

"What's wrong?" Mrs. Chang asked, rounding the corner.

"Bailey just found out there's a film festival here this
weekend and the streets will be swarming with stars." Kate
smiled sweetly and pushed up her glasses.

Mrs. Chang put her arm around Bailey. "I hate to break
this to you, but we're going home on Thursday."

"Some of the stars may come early. I've got to be ready,"
Bailey replied breathlessly. "Kate, will you be my manager?"

"Of course," Kate answered.

Bailey eyed her friend's mismatched outfit. "But we may
need to work on your wardrobe."

Kate smoothed her clothes out with her hand. "What's
wrong with this?" Kate asked.

"Nothing for your everyday girl look," Bailey said. "But if you want to be a Hollywood agent, it doesn't quite cut it."

"*Hollywood* agent?" Kate scrunched up her nose. "You're from Peoria, Illinois, and I'm from Philadelphia, Pennsylvania!"

"But you have to dress for success." Bailey waved her arm with a flair. "You have to act the part of who you *want* to be, not just who you are."

Biscuit yawned loudly.

"Hmm. Maybe I'm not ready for this Hollywood agent thing."

"Of course you are!" Bailey patted Kate on the back. "You just have to believe in yourself."

Suddenly, a commotion outside drew Bailey and Kate to the store window. People scattered from the streets, revealing two enormous elk standing on their hind legs pawing at each other as if they were boxing. When Mrs. Chang and Trina hurried over to see what was going on, Mrs. Chang put her arms protectively around the girls.

"Must be two males fighting over a female," Bailey overheard a man say.

"But they usually do that in the hills, not right here in the middle of town!" said another.

"I see Justin and Joe out there!" Bailey yelled and pulled away from her mother.

"Bailey! Don't go out there!" Mrs. Chang screamed.

Biscuit barked wildly, each bark almost lifting him off his feet.

Bailey flung open the door and as she did, the elk bolted toward the hills, leaving only dust to prove their presence. Coughing, Bailey tried to spot Justin and Joe. Kate, Mom, and Trina appeared at her side.

"I don't see them!" Bailey wailed, beginning to wheeze. She pulled her inhaler from her pocket and breathed in the asthma medication.

As the dust settled, people began talking excitedly. No one had been hurt, just shaken. Bailey, from the corner of her eye, saw two figures running down the street.

"There they go!" she said. "Justin! Joe!" she called. But the two kept on running.

"Guess they're in a hurry to get out of here," Kate said.

"I can't blame them," Trina replied. "Are we ready to move on? I looked at all the rocks I can stand."

"I guess." Bailey gave a longing glance back at the rock shop. "I didn't get anything for my collection, but I'm not exactly in the mood anymore. I think I'm ready to go back to the hotel."

"I'm more than ready," Mrs. Chang said with a shiver. "Too many elk around here for my taste."

"Look at this," Kate said. "This sign says there's a free shuttle a few blocks down the street that can take us back."

"Mom, can Kate and I take the shuttle back?" Bailey begged.

"I suppose," Mrs. Chang answered. "Just stay on the sidewalk and keep your eyes open for running elk."

"I doubt there will be any more since those two just went through," Bailey said. "But we'll be careful."

Mrs. Chang and Trina went back to their car and the girls walked to the shuttle stop.

"I wonder what made the elk come into town like that?" Bailey thought aloud.

"Me, too."

"I hate to say it, but it almost seemed like Justin and Joe were ahead of the elk, like they were leading them here." Bailey grimaced at the thought.

"That doesn't seem likely," Kate said. "They were probably just at that end of the street when it all began."

"Yeah, you're probably right."

When the girls neared the shuttle stop, Bailey stuck her arm out in front of Kate to stop her. "Look!" Bailey pointed to the bench at the shuttle stop. "It's them!"

"Let's go!" Kate took off running.

The boys didn't see the girls until Bailey poked Justin's arm.

"What'ja do that for?" Justin snarled.

"We wanted to surprise you." Bailey flashed her sweetest smile.

"Are you guys okay?" Kate asked. "We saw you running from the elk."

"Yeah, we're okay." Justin studied his tennis shoes.

"How was your hike?" Bailey asked.

"Hike?" Joe said.

"I thought you hiked here," Bailey said.

"Oh yeah, we did," Joe said. "But we're taking the shuttle back."

"Where's your hiking stick?" Kate noticed Justin's jacket was unzipped all the way down and hanging open.

"Hiking stick?" Justin's eyebrows descended like dark clouds on a mountain, confusion filling his eyes.

"Yeah, you said the long thing you were carrying in your coat at the hotel was your hiking stick." Bailey crossed her arms and waited for an answer.

"Oh, that!" Justin laughed as if he'd just been told the world's funniest joke. "We left it on our way down from the hill. Got tired of carrying it."

"Hmm," Bailey said, hardly convinced. "Here comes the shuttle."

•—•—•

Back at the room, Bailey sat on the floor with her suitcase and sorted through her clothes looking for just the right outfit for her "Hollywood Moment." A pile of rejected items surrounded her as she pulled out another shirt. "Mom, would you let Kate and me go hiking on one of the trails by ourselves?"

Trina strolled by her and rolled her eyes but held her tongue.

"Only if you promise to stay on the trail," Mrs. Chang replied.

"We will, won't we, Kate?" Bailey tossed a tie-dyed

51

shirt on the floor.

Kate nodded her approval. "And Biscuit could be our guide dog."

"Let's try it tomorrow!" Bailey said, suddenly feeling she'd just been set free.

"Tomorrow's the Elkfest," Kate reminded her. "We'll have to go the next day."

"Shucks," Bailey whispered, her voice registering her dismay. "I wanted to look for that 'hiking stick' Justin left behind."

"Exactly what I was thinking," Kate said with a nod. "We'll just have to pray it's still there when we go."

"There!" Bailey said, holding up a red long-sleeved T-shirt with rhinestones that spelled "sweet," and a pair of new jeans with flowered embroidery down the leg. "I have my Hollywood outfit figured out for wearing to the Elkfest tomorrow. You never know, there may be a talent scout there for the film festival, too!"

●—●—●

That night, Bailey could hardly wait for lights-out in their room. "Hurry up, Trina!" she ordered. "How long can it take for you to brush your teeth and wash your face?"

Trina stuck her head out from the bathroom, growling with her foamy, white mouth.

"Patience, Bales, patience," Mr. Chang said calmly from behind a business report.

"We never hear the children of the night until the lights

are out and everyone's quiet," Bailey tried to explain. "We need to get to bed so we can listen."

Kate was already beneath the covers, which she'd tucked snugly under her chin. Biscuit puttered around her feet, making his bed just right. He plopped down with a giant sigh just as Trina finally emerged fresh-faced and ready for bed.

"Okay, lights out!" Bailey said. Mrs. Chang flipped the switch and the room went dark. Silence flooded the room like billowing smoke, filling every corner until Bailey could hardly breathe. "I don't hear anything, do you?" she whispered to Kate.

"Uh-uh."

"Maybe no one's out there to trip the switch." Sweat beaded on Bailey's upper lip. A door in the hallway creaked then slammed. Bailey raised her head to listen even harder, if that was possible.

"We'll just have to wait it out," Kate whispered.

Bailey nodded in the dark and lay perfectly still. Then she heard it.

Elkfest!

A muffled, high-pitched giggle seeped into the room. Bailey and Kate sprang from their bed like jack-in-the-boxes.

"We'll be back in a few," Bailey said breathlessly. She grabbed her robe, then her cell phone for light. Biscuit let out a yip but then settled back into his cozy blanket.

"He must be getting used to us jumping out of bed," Kate said softly.

When Bailey opened the door, Trina groaned and pulled the covers over her eyes as the wedge of light poured in from the hall. Kate followed Bailey to the door but then took the lead once it closed behind them. They hurried to the speaker they'd seen in the hall earlier and waited. Nothing.

"Something has to be tripping this thing to set it off." Kate looked around.

A ding alerted the girls that someone was about to get off the elevator. The doors opened, and a middle-aged couple emerged and went to their room at the far end of the hall in the opposite direction from the girls. Their door closed with a bang.

Hee-hee-heeeeee!

Bailey saw Kate's eyes widen and a grin spread across her friend's face. The laugh had come from the speaker above them. The two jogged down the hall. Bailey looked in all the potted plants in the hallway for a switch of some kind that the couple might have brushed against. Kate got on all fours and felt the carpet from the elevator to the couple's room.

"I found something!" she said in a loud whisper. "Feel right here."

Bailey joined Kate on her hands and knees and ran her hand along the carpet. "A bump!" she said.

"I think it's the switch that turns on the ghost children's laughter. It comes on when someone steps on it."

"Let's try it." Bailey scrunched up her shoulders. "I can't wait to tell Alex about this since she's the one who told us to look for a switch." She stood and stepped on the bump.

Almost a full minute of silence passed. "It didn't work!" Bailey moaned.

Hee-hee-heeeeee!

"It's on a delay!"

"Kate! You're a genius!" Bailey hugged her friend.

"They must have delayed the ghost recording so when people hear the children laughing and look out into the hall, whoever tripped the switch would have had enough time to get to their room."

"Yeah, so no one would be there when they checked!" Bailey gave Kate a high five.

"Well, that solves that one!" Kate said.

"Now if we can just figure out why the elk are going nuts."

"Yeah, that's a tougher one to pin down."

Bailey scratched her head. "Maybe Sydney will have discovered some information about elk behavior that will help us. Let's call her tomorrow."

"We'd better get back," Kate said.

They returned to their room, the sound of *Hee-hee-heeeeee!* echoing in their heads.

The next morning, Bailey awoke to a deep, reverberating sound that rose quickly to a high-pitched squeal and was followed by a series of low grunts. Biscuit sat up, ears twitching. Bailey rubbed her eyes. "What was *that*?" Mr. and Mrs. Chang were already up and dressed. Trina obviously slept through anything.

"Not another ghost, I hope," Mrs. Chang said with a smirk.

"Sounds like a wounded elephant," Kate said, stretching.

"I think it's coming from outside." Bailey went to the window to investigate. "There's a guy out here blowing some kind of horn."

"I know what it is," Mr. Chang said. "I read about it in the newspaper this morning. Today is the start of the Elkfest, and he's bugling like an elk to begin the festivities."

"Oh yeah!" Bailey said. "We saw a poster about that in town yesterday and we picked up a flyer that told all about it. We thought you should enter the bugling contest, Dad." She cast a mischievous look his way.

"Sure thing. I'll get right on that," Mr. Chang teased back. "It would be fun to watch some of it, though," he admitted.

"Do you have meetings today?" Kate asked.

"Just one. After that, I'm free." Mr. Chang looked at his watch. "I'd better get going. I hope to be back around ten. We can go into town then if you'd like."

"Yeah, if Trina ever gets up!" Bailey yelled, hoping to wake her sister.

Mrs. Chang gave her a look. "You didn't make it any too easy for her to sleep last night with your ghost capers," she said. "Did you figure anything out?"

Bailey and Kate filled Mrs. Chang in on how the ghost children's voices were activated. "Pretty smart of you to figure all that out," Mrs. Chang said. "I'm impressed."

"We need to send an e-mail to the other CCGs to let them know." Bailey turned on the laptop. "Hopefully, they'll have some elk info for us."

Bailey opened her e-mail and found a note from Sydney. Kate read over her shoulder.

Hi. An elk's #1 defense is his sense of smell. He can spook at the scent of a human as far as a mile away.

Hunters have to keep checking the wind to make sure it isn't blowing their scent toward where the elk gather.

Elk also have excellent hearing and can be spooked by a car or an ATV miles away. Of course I'm talking about wild elk. Sounds like the elk in Estes Park are used to people and vehicles, unless they possibly feel threatened by someone and remember their scent.

"That's interesting," Bailey said. "Maybe the elk are catching the scent of someone who's been mean to them and that's what's making them charge."

"Maybe," Kate replied. "Anyway, it gives us something to start with. If there's another incident, we'll have to keep our eyes open for any similar circumstances."

●—●—●

Bailey stepped out of the car at the Elkfest in her favorite jeans with flowers embroidered down the sides of each leg and sequins in the centers of each flower. Her long-sleeved red, rhinestoned T-shirt had thumbholes at the end of each cuff. Large white sunglasses and shiny pink lip gloss completed her Hollywood outfit. Kate, unaffected by Bailey's pleas that she dress like an agent, wore green plaid pants and a Hawaiian print shirt.

Bailey felt the same excitement when she looked around at the Elkfest as she did her first time at the circus.

The sweet aroma of hot Indian fry bread mingled with corn dogs and cotton candy. Elk roamed freely among the crowd, eating the food people dropped. Live country-western music filled the air and a festive mood settled over the town.

"When's the bugling contest?" Bailey asked, looking for movie stars.

Mr. Chang looked at a schedule he'd picked up. "At one o'clock."

Bailey looked at her watch. "It's only eleven thirty now."

"Maybe we should get some lunch, then head over that way so we get good seats," Mr. Chang suggested.

"Hey, there are the Perkinses!" Mrs. Chang said. She waved to the family.

"Hi, Dory," Mrs. Perkins said to Mrs. Chang. "What do you think of the Elkfest?"

"It's terrific! We're interested in the bugling contest, but we see it isn't until one o'clock," Mr. Chang told them.

"Yeah, they always have it in the afternoon," Mr. Perkins said. "My dad is in the competition again this year." He motioned to Justin and Joe's grandpa. "He won it a couple years ago."

"No kidding!" Mr. Chang said.

"Now we'll have someone to cheer for." Bailey wished she could turn a flip like Alex could. She would have done one on the spot.

"We'll see if I'm worth cheering for in a couple hours,

won't we?" Grandpa Perkins winked at Bailey. "I appreciate your enthusiasm and support."

Bailey turned to Justin and Joe. "You must be excited to see your grandpa in the contest, huh?"

"Sure," Joe said. "He'll win, I just know it." He smiled at his grandpa, and Bailey thought it was the happiest she'd ever seen Joe. Justin shrugged and kicked a rock in the dirt.

"We were just getting ready to eat a bite of lunch," Mrs. Chang said. "Would you like to join us?"

"We can't eat until after Grandpa's contest is over," Justin glowered at the Changs. "He can't bugle on a full stomach."

"Oh, I see," Mrs. Chang said, hesitation marking her words as she looked uncertainly at Justin.

"Actually, we had a late breakfast so we could eat lunch later after Dad's big performance." Mr. Perkins's face seemed a bit redder than usual. "But thanks anyway."

"Good luck on the contest!" Bailey said as the families parted. "We'll be rooting for you!"

"Thanks!" Grandpa Perkins replied. "I'll need all the help I can get!"

The Changs found a hot dog stand and ordered five hot dogs and drinks. The aroma had tempted Bailey since they arrived. She loaded her dog with ketchup, mustard, and relish.

While they ate, they watched Native American dancers perform. Bailey was enthralled by the unusual dance style—

the silent tap, tap, tapping of their moccasin-clad feet and the leaning and swaying of their bodies. They moved to the beat of a tom-tom drum, its leather top being struck hard, then soft, to make different rhythms and sounds.

A medium-skinned man with a long ponytail of black hair streaked with gray sang in his Native American language. The young dancers especially impressed Bailey. Some of them looked much younger than her. She clapped hard when their performance ended.

"Trina and I are going to run to the restroom before going to the bugling contest," Mrs. Chang told the girls. "Do you want to come?"

"I'm okay," Bailey said.

"Me, too," Kate agreed.

"That sounds like a good idea," Mr. Chang added. "You girls stay right here until we get back."

Kate grabbed Bailey's arm when the family left. "Look!"

The Perkins family was down the street, and Justin and Joe appeared to be telling their parents something. Then the boys ran toward one of the hills surrounding the town.

"Looks like they're going to do some hill climbing." Bailey frowned. "I wonder if they picked up their 'walking stick' from the area they hiked yesterday."

"You mean *gun*?" Kate snorted. "Those guys are either avid hikers or they are up to something. What time is it?"

Bailey checked her watch. "Twelve fifteen."

"Their hike will have to be short, or they'll miss their

grandpa's bugling performance."

"And Joe seemed excited about seeing it." Bailey remembered Joe's unexpected smile. "I don't think he'd want to miss it."

"Justin, however, is another matter." Kate pushed her glasses up. She dug in her pocket and pulled out her camera-pen. Holding it horizontally, she twisted the pointed end to zoom in as close as possible. Justin and Joe's image got larger on the metal clip. She quickly clicked the end. Bailey joined in with her camera-watch.

"Between the two of us, we should have some good shots to share with the Camp Club Girls." Kate returned her pen to her pocket.

"Are we ready?" Mr. Chang said when the family met up again.

"Ready!" the girls shouted in unison.

"Let's go cheer Grandpa Perkins on!"

The Changs sat in the grass near the front and sipped on their sodas. A magician entertained the crowd gathering for the bugling contest.

"I need a volunteer," the magician said. "Who will help me?"

Bailey's hand was up like a rocket.

"You, there, in the red sparkly shirt." The magician pointed to Bailey.

"He's pointing at you, Bailey!" Kate pushed her friend to her feet. "If there are talent scouts out there, they'll all see you on stage. It could be your big break!"

Bailey ran up to the stage, her family applauding her all the way.

The magician asked Bailey her name and age. Then he looked confused. "Hmm. That's unusual," he said.

"What?" Bailey asked.

"You seem to have something on the back of your shirt."

"I do?" Bailey twisted to see.

The magician reached behind her and pulled out a bouquet of flowers. "Oh, I'm sorry. I hope I didn't spoil the surprise you were hiding for your mother."

Bailey squealed and clapped.

The magician handed the flowers to Mrs. Chang. "Let's hear it for my lovely assistant, Bailey! Thank you for your help, miss."

Bailey curtsied grandly and took her seat. "Do you think anyone famous saw me?" she asked Kate.

"If they were here, they totally saw you," she replied.

Soon, the contest began. A panel of judges sat in front of the stage and took notes on each contestant's bugling ability. Bailey scanned the crowd a short time later and spotted the Perkins family, including Justin and Joe, sitting on the other side of the bugling area.

"I guess they made it back in time," Bailey whispered to Kate. She nodded in the boys' direction.

"Guess so," Kate said. "And Justin actually looks almost happy."

"Amazing!" Bailey joked.

Grandpa Perkins's name was announced, and he went to the microphone. "I've been in this bugling contest five years running and only won once, two years ago. But this is the first time I've ever had two cheering sections." He waved his arm toward his family and then the Changs. They all yelled their loudest. Grandpa gave them an informal salute then cleared his throat and got down to business. He let out two low, resonant tones that quickly rose to a high-pitched squeal, followed by three deep grunts. He sounded just like one of the elk!

The crowd went wild. Even the elk in the park stopped and looked. Grandpa bowed before waving and taking his seat on the stage with the other contestants.

Bailey clapped wildly. "Grandpa Perkins was fantastic!"

Kate nodded. "I bet he wins the grand prize."

The bugling contest continued, but after about the fifth person, Bailey thought she felt a slight tremor. She looked at Kate, who looked back at her, questions in her eyes. The shaking increased and soon people were on their feet running and yelling, "Stampede!"

Elk ran through the crowd on their long, knobby legs, more elk than Bailey had ever seen at one time before. Dust flew and parents snatched small children to safety. When the rumbling and shaking ended, Bailey noticed some people lying on the ground injured.

"The Perkinses! Where are they?" Bailey wondered

aloud. As much as she didn't like Justin and Joe, she didn't want any of them to get hurt. The dust cleared and she caught sight of them. "There they are! By the stage."

Mr. Perkins was helping a shaken Grandpa Perkins off the stage. "They look like they're okay," Kate said. "We're lucky we weren't hurt."

Bailey listened to conversations around her.

"What do you think caused the elk to run through town this time?"

"I bet it was the bugling contest. Probably drew them right in."

"They've never done that before."

"Had some mighty good buglers this year."

"They're probably nervous with all these people around."

"They're trying to protect their young."

"Protect their young? They were born in May, five months ago."

"I think they're aggressive because it's mating season."

"Could be. Peak mating is September and October."

"But they've never been this aggressive in mating season before. Something got them stirred up."

"Seems like they show up only to charge lately. They don't roam around as freely as they once did."

"True enough. And they seem to come out more in the evenings than they used to."

"Where did they come from?"

"From that hill," one said, pointing to where Bailey and

Kate had seen Justin and Joe hiking.

"That's the opposite direction from when they came out of the woods last time."

Bailey looked at Kate as they took in all the talk. "What do you think, Kate?"

"I don't know," she said thoughtfully. "I think we need to talk to the other girls. Seems when we work together, things come together faster."

"Two heads—or six—are better than one!" Bailey agreed.

As the people gathered, leaders announced that the bugling contest would resume in an hour and the winner would be declared shortly after that. The Changs walked over to where the Perkins family stood.

"Everyone all right here?" Mr. Chang asked.

"Yes, a bit shaken, but not injured," Mr. Perkins answered. "Your family okay?"

"We're fine, too," Mr. Chang replied.

"Mr. Perkins," Bailey said to Grandpa, "you were awesome!"

"Yeah, you sounded like a real elk!" Kate agreed.

"I bet you're going to win." Bailey grinned as if she'd just won a prize herself.

"Of course he'll win," Justin said, surprising Bailey. "No *tourist* should win the local contest."

"Well, now, I wouldn't say that," Grandpa said, patting his grandson's back. "The best bugler should win, wherever he's from."

"A tourist doesn't know the elk bugle as well as the locals," Justin maintained. "They should just give up and go home."

Bailey almost laughed until she saw how serious Justin was. No hint of a smile crossed his face, no look of pride in his grandpa. Just the usual anger. Was it her imagination or was that jab at tourists targeted at her and her family?

"Come on, Bailey," Kate said, hooking her arm through her friend's. "I'm so sure Grandpa Perkins is going to win, we may as well go see some more of the Elkfest."

Bailey glanced at her mother. "Is it okay, Mom?"

"Sure, go have fun," Mrs. Chang replied.

Target Practice

When Bailey and Kate returned from the Elkfest that evening, they made a conference call to the other Camp Club Girls. Leaving Trina to watch TV in the hotel room, the two friends sat on an overstuffed couch in the lobby. Biscuit, on his leash, sat quietly between them. After all the girls were on the line, Bailey explained the children of the night mystery. Kate supplemented the story with technical details.

"You were right about the hidden switch, Alex," Bailey told her. "Kate found it under the hallway carpet."

"But what we hadn't counted on," Kate added, "was that it was on a timer, so it didn't go off immediately when stepped on."

"Wow! You guys are awesome!" Alex exclaimed. Bailey imagined her doing a backflip with her typical cheerleader enthusiasm. "Scooby Doo would be proud. Next thing you know they'll be asking you to be on their show!"

McKenzie giggled. "Now *that* I'd like to see! Bailey and Kate as cartoon characters!"

"Anything to report on the elk research, Syd?" Bailey asked.

"Yeah. Hold on. I've found out a few things."

Bailey heard papers rustling, and then Sydney continued.

"The elk in the Estes Park Rocky Mountain area are called wapiti elk. Wapiti means 'white rump' in the Shawnee Indian language."

Bailey laughed. "Yep. That's them, all right."

"Like I mentioned before, adult elk have an awesome sense of smell, but they also have excellent hearing and can run up to thirty-five miles an hour. They're well equipped to avoid the cougars and bears that prey on them. Strong animals like elk don't need much cover except during extreme weather, to avoid hunters, or when they're harassed."

"Harassed?" McKenzie asked.

"You know, if people or other animals bother them," Sydney explained. "They're very social animals and live in herds most of the year. They're mostly active at dawn and dusk, but when it gets hot or when they're harassed, elk may become more active at night. When they're not being hunted, elk get along well with humans so lawns and golf courses become some of their favorite restaurants."

The girls giggled and Biscuit joined in with happy barks.

Sydney continued reading. "September and October are good months to observe them because the boy elk—or bulls, as they're called—are battling over the girl elk, so they aren't as worried about being seen. You'll hear the bull's bugle usually near dusk or dawn. You should be careful around the male elk during mating season, especially in areas where they're used to being around people, because they tend to be more aggressive."

"So maybe it *is* because of mating season that the elk have been acting so strange," Kate said. "We heard someone say that at the Elkfest today."

"But from hearing the townspeople talk, it seems they're more aggressive than usual this year." Bailey sighed.

"Sydney said they become more active at night if they're harassed," Elizabeth added.

"Good point," Bailey said. "We overheard someone mention that after the elk stampede today."

"But who or what is harassing them?" McKenzie asked.

"That's the question." Kate stroked Biscuit, her face thoughtful.

Silence filled the phone line for a moment.

"Not to change the subject, but have you seen those boys anymore?" Alex asked.

"Yeah, we've seen them a couple of times," Bailey answered. "They went on a hike yesterday."

"With a very unusual walking stick," Kate added, concern clouding her face.

"Oh yeah." Bailey's eyes sought Kate's. "We didn't get a good look at it, but Justin, the older boy, had something hidden in his coat. When we asked him about it, he said it was his walking stick."

"But it looked like it was made out of metal," Kate chimed in, "and though it *was* sort of long, it was still too short to be a walking stick."

"Then we saw them out the window as they left the hotel and walked to a wooded area. Justin's walking stick was in plain view by then and it turns out. . ." Bailey paused dramatically, ". . .it was a gun!"

The other girls gasped in unison.

"What kind of gun?" Elizabeth asked.

"It looked like an air pellet gun or whatever those are called," Kate said.

"It's called an airsoft gun," Sydney said. "My older brother has one. It's kind of like a BB gun, but smaller, and the pellets can sting but not do serious damage."

"But get this," Bailey's voice rose in excitement. "When they came back, they didn't have it with them. When we asked them about it, they said they got tired of carrying it and left it behind."

"Well, they said they left their walking stick behind, since they just claimed they had a walking stick," Kate said.

"Yeah, right!" McKenzie said. "That doesn't seem likely."

"Bailey, you and Kate have to be careful around those two," Elizabeth warned. "Avoid them if you can. First Corinthians 15:33 says, 'Do not be misled: Bad company corrupts good character.' Don't take any unnecessary chances."

"We won't," Kate assured her.

Bailey stood and stretched. "We'd better get to bed. But

if any of you think of anything that could help us, let us know. And Sydney, thanks for the great info on elk. Keep up the good work."

—•——•——•—

The next morning, Bailey and Kate started out on their hike with Biscuit, taking their secret cameras, water, cell phones, binoculars, and some trail mix. Both girls wore hoodies to ward off the early morning chill.

Rather than taking the free shuttle, Bailey and Kate decided to hike into town. They passed the rock shop and lots of cute restaurants they hoped Bailey's parents would take them to before their vacation ended. The girls lingered outside the fudge and ice cream shop, their mouths watering. They enjoyed seeing the sleepy town wake up, its stores just opening.

"Hey, look! A miniature golf course!" Kate pushed her glasses up.

"Want to play a round before we head up the hill?" Bailey asked.

"Sure!" Kate reached down and picked up her dog. "Reminds me of the day we found Biscuit at Camp Discovery!"

The two grinned and rubbed the wiggling fur ball.

"You were so cute," Kate cooed to him.

"And dirty and stinky!" Bailey plugged her nose at the memory.

Kate covered the dog's ears. "Don't you listen to her.

You've always been a prince." She set Biscuit back down.

Bailey paid the man at the counter for the round of golf and they chose clubs that were just their sizes.

"What do you think Justin and Joe are up to today?" Bailey asked.

"Probably still sleeping." Kate stepped up to the first hole and teed off.

Bailey looked at her watch. "I guess it *is* only nine o'clock." She took her turn.

"Look at that huge elk!" Kate pointed to the street. Biscuit barked and pranced around Kate's feet.

Just as Bailey turned to look, the elk raised his head and let out a shrill bugle.

"Wow! He sounds just like Grandpa Perkins!" Bailey said seriously and then laughed at how it must have sounded. "From what we just heard, I bet he won that bugling contest yesterday. We'll have to find out today."

Bailey and Kate moved to the next hole, a miniature Rocky Mountain peak with tunnels for the ball to go through in the middle of the base, and one on either side.

Kate stuck out her neck and squinted through her glasses.

"What are you looking at?" Bailey asked when she realized her friend was looking into the distance rather than at the golf tunnels.

"I think I'm looking at Justin and Joe," Kate replied, pointing toward the hill they hoped to hike later. She pushed her glasses up and squinted to get a better look.

Bailey's head swung in the direction Kate's finger pointed. She snatched the binoculars out of their case and peered through them. Focusing in, she found the boys. "That's them all right, and it looks like they got to the 'walking stick' before we did."

"Really?" Kate sounded disappointed, but then her voice perked up. "Can you see the 'walking stick' clearly?"

"*Very* clearly, and we were right—that's no walking stick."

Kate grabbed the binoculars from her friend and looked. "No, it isn't. That is definitely a gun, and it looks like they're doing some target practice."

"What are they shooting at?" Now it was Bailey's turn to squint.

"Looks like they have empty soda cans lined up on a tree stump," Kate said. "It's hard to tell since the trees are so thick there." Kate lowered the binoculars.

"So we were right," Bailey repeated, her hands on her hips.

Kate nodded. "They were lying, just as we thought."

"Maybe we're jumping to conclusions," Bailey said solemnly. "Just because they're shooting a gun doesn't make them bad people. As long as they're being careful and shooting at things like cans. And it's probably an airsoft gun like Sydney told us about—the kind that just shoots little plastic pellets."

"But why would they try to cover it up by lying?" Kate pointed her golf club at Bailey. "That's what makes it suspicious."

Bailey sighed. "I suppose you're right. Although many people don't approve of kids using even plastic pellet guns."

"Let's hurry up and finish this golf game and get over to that hill," Kate said. "Maybe we'll see what they're up to."

"Yeah," Bailey agreed. "It's your turn."

Bailey and Kate finished their round of golf and hurried to the hill, where elk and bighorn sheep roamed around its base. Biscuit ran ahead of them, causing the big animals to scatter. The air smelled crisp and fall-like, red and gold leaves crunching under their feet as they walked.

"It smells so good out here!" Kate said as she stared at a towering pine.

"If nothing else, maybe we can learn some more about the elk's behavior while we're out here," Bailey said. She moved close to a pine tree and sniffed the bark.

"What are you doing?" Kate looked at her friend like she'd gone crazy.

"Smelling the bark," Bailey answered matter-of-factly.

"Well, I can see that. But why?"

"Come see for yourself." Bailey motioned her over. "Sniff."

Kate looked around then put her nose close to the tree and inhaled. Biscuit came back and sniffed all around the tree, too.

"Well?" Bailey asked.

"Smells like vanilla!" Kate cried

"See? Aren't you glad you tried?" Bailey took another sniff. "Sometimes I can't decide if it smells like vanilla or butterscotch, but either way it smells good."

"Where'd you learn that?" Kate asked.

"Sydney, of course," Bailey answered. "She showed me at camp the first day she and I went out hiking."

"I should have guessed Syd would have taught you that."

The two walked on. Biscuit trotted alongside the trail just a few feet ahead.

"What's that?" Bailey took a few steps off the trail and stopped by a bathtub-size, shallow hole in the ground.

"I don't know, but it smells awful!" Kate covered her nose and mouth with her hands. Biscuit scampered into the sunken earth, sniffing furiously.

Bailey took a few steps closer. "It's so muddy I can hardly get any closer."

"Biscuit's going to be a mess!"

"He already is." Bailey bent down and looked at the huge indentation. "There are light brown hairs in the mud. And look at all these tracks around it."

Kate stooped to look at the four-inch footprints that looked like a long heart shape cut down the middle. "Do you think these are elk tracks?"

Bailey shrugged. "We'll have to check on the Internet."

"Or ask Sydney."

"Let's get some pictures of it and we can send them to her to see." Bailey aimed her camera-watch at the indentation and Kate pulled out her camera-pen.

"These hairs sure look the same color as elk fur," Kate said.

"Come on. Let's keep going." Bailey stood and walked back to the trail, trying not to sink into the mud. "Must be so muddy because of that pond over there."

The girls looked at a small pool of water almost hidden by reeds. It sat just yards beyond the smelly indentation.

"Let's go, boy," Kate called to Biscuit. The mud-covered dog plodded his way out of the bog to her side.

"I guess today we'll find out who won the bugling contest." Bailey kicked some fall leaves that covered the trail.

"If anyone can bugle better than Grandpa Perkins, he's probably part elk!"

Bailey suddenly stopped and listened.

"Wha—?" Kate began, but Bailey held her hand up to stop her and put her finger to her lips.

Bailey tiptoed to the right of the trail and hid behind a tree, motioning Kate to join her. When Kate reached her, she whispered, "I think I hear Justin's and Joe's voices."

Kate nodded silently. She picked up Biscuit and reattached his leash, his muddy feet leaving marks all over her light pink hoodie. She didn't dare complain or make a sound.

The girls stayed still as stones but heard nothing more.

"Apparently they've moved farther up the hill from when we saw them earlier. Let's keep going," Bailey whispered. "But stay off to the side of the trail so if they come down this way, they won't see us."

"We told your mom we'd stay on the trail," Kate reminded her.

"We'll be right beside it," Bailey said. "We'll keep it in sight. She just didn't want us wandering and getting lost."

The girls crept silently, like spies, hopping from behind one tree to the next. The boys' voices grew louder.

"Look over there," Bailey exclaimed.

Kate nodded. Justin and Joe had moved their target practice off the trail.

"I can barely hear them," Kate said. "And I don't have a clear view of them."

Bailey scurried to the next tree, which took her several feet closer to the boys. Kate followed carefully. She pulled out her camera-pen and snapped a few pictures of the boys. Bailey did the same with her camera-watch, just for good measure. Biscuit caught sight of what the girls were looking at and a low growl rumbled in his throat.

"Shhhh," Kate said softly as she scratched the dog's head to try to calm him.

Justin stopped mid-aim and looked around as if he'd heard something. Then he refocused his aim at the pop cans lined on a tree stump.

Bailey strained to hear what they said.

"We'll show them," Justin said to his younger brother. "We'll have them so scared they never come back!" With that, he pulled his trigger and a loud pop rang out.

Biscuit barked and leaped from Kate's arms. He ran in the boys' direction, leash dragging behind him.

"What in the wo—" Justin turned and saw Biscuit flying

at him, barking wildly.

"It's those girls' dog!" Joe yelled. He spun in circles, eyes searching the woods.

"Biscuit!" Kate jumped from behind the tree and raced after the dog, with Bailey close behind.

"Get that dog away from me!" shouted Justin.

"Biscuit! Come here!" Kate screamed.

The girls reached the boys just as Justin raised his airsoft gun and pointed it at Biscuit.

Lost!

"NOOO!" Kate shrieked.

The gun went off. Biscuit yelped and darted into the woods.

"Biscuit!" Kate rushed through the trees after her dog.

Bailey strode squarely to confront Justin, whose gun hung limp in his hand. "Why did you do that?" she demanded, tears stinging her eyes.

"He was going to attack me!" Justin yelled.

"He was barking around your feet! If he wanted to attack you, he would have jumped at you."

"Well, I wasn't going to wait to find out." Justin ran his hand through his short hair, his face flushed. "It would have been too late to do anything by then." He looked at his younger brother, who stood dazed nearby. "You okay, Joe?"

"I—I think so," he stammered.

"Let's get out of here before that dog comes back and attacks us again." Justin set his gun on the safety setting and stuffed it into his jacket as Joe gathered their targets and supplies.

Bailey wanted to grab the gun and knock both boys senseless with it. Instead she turned and dashed into the woods. "Kate?" she called. The wind in the trees was her only reply. "Kate!" Nothing.

Bailey looked back and realized she could no longer see the trail they'd been on. She stood for a few minutes, trying to push down her fear. *What should I do?* All she could think of was Kate and Biscuit, but she didn't know how to find them. In the shadows of the towering pines, the air felt chilly, even with her hoodie on.

Which way should I go? Bailey looked around her again. *I can't think!*

"Kate!" Still no reply.

Bailey sucked in a deep breath and let it out slowly. *Help me think, God. Show me what to do.* She tucked her icy hands into her hoodie pockets and fingered her cell phone. *That's it! Thanks, God!* Snatching it out, she dialed Kate. Thank heavens she could pick up a signal. One ring. Two rings.

"Hello?"

"Kate! Thank goodness! Where are you?"

"I'm not sure."

Bailey heard Kate's voice tremble. "Did you find Biscuit?"

"Yeah, he's here with me."

"Is he okay?"

"I think so. I looked over him and didn't see any injuries. I guess he was just spooked by the noise of the gun."

Bailey closed her eyes and sighed. "I about let Justin have it when you and Biscuit disappeared into the woods. He claimed Biscuit was about to attack him. I nearly decked him, even if he is bigger than me."

Kate laughed. "Well, I'm glad you held yourself back. That's all we need is for him to say Biscuit attacked him and then you assaulted him."

The girls grew silent. "Bailey, we have to find each other and get back to the trail."

"I don't know which way to go." Bailey's voice rose, fear once again curling within.

"Hang on a second."

Bailey could hear rustling, as if Kate were looking for something. "Here it is."

"What?"

"My mini-GPS. It's a trial product my dad brought home from work one day. What better time to try it out than now?"

"Trial product? GPS units have been around awhile."

"But this one is tiny. It fits into the palm of my hand. I can clip it onto my belt if I want."

"That's fantastic!"

"Let's see, I'll put in Estes Park, Colorado, and see what it brings up." Kate punched in the city and state. "It worked! Now I just have to zoom in to find that street we were on."

"I'm glad you're the one trying to figure this out," Bailey said. "I'm directionally challenged."

"Here we go," Kate said. "Looks like we walked north to get to this hill from town. The sun was to our right, so that must be east since it rose only a few hours earlier, right?"

Bailey relaxed. "You're starting to sound like Sydney!"

"So to get back we need to go south, so the sun is to our left."

Bailey looked up and shielded her eyes from the sun. "I'll hang up and yell for you. Hopefully, you'll hear me as you get closer. Then we can look for the trail together from here."

"Okay," Kate said, "but if I don't hear you soon, I'm calling you back."

"Deal." Bailey stuffed her phone back in her pocket and yelled, "Kate! Kate, I'm over here!"

She yelled for what seemed like a full minute, stopping only to listen briefly for an answer. A cool breeze swirled dry leaves around her feet, and she zipped her mud-splotched hoodie clear to the neck.

"Kate!" Leaves crunched behind her and Bailey swung around. "Kate?" No answer, but the crunching drew closer. "Kate, if that's you, you'd better answer me!" Silence. "Kate, this isn't funny!"

From behind a clump of trees, a huge elk with enormous antlers stuck out his head and looked at Bailey. She froze, not sure if the elk would charge or if he was as afraid as she was. They stood, eyes locked, neither one moving a muscle. Finally, the elk seemed satisfied that the girl meant no harm and munched on a nearby shrub. Bailey exhaled a breath she didn't realize she'd been holding and inched forward to get a better view of the elk.

Suddenly Bailey was startled by her cell phone ringing. "Kate? I'm watching a big elk eat. You should see him!"

"You're supposed to be calling for me, remember?"

"I did, but then the elk scared me and I was afraid to make much noise."

Bailey heard rustling again and turned to look. The elk turned his head, too, ears twitching. "Kate! Over here!"

At the sound of Bailey's voice, the elk turned toward her and narrowed his eyes. He lowered his head, those gigantic antlers pointing in her direction, then took a few steps toward her. Hardly daring to take a breath, Bailey froze. Images of charging elk filled her mind.

Biscuit sniffed the air and leaped out of Kate's arms, barking wildly. The tiny dog ran at the towering elk, who seemed momentarily confused by all the excitement. He tried to keep his eye on the dog prancing at his feet, one minute in front of him and the next behind. In apparent exasperation, the elk turned and lumbered off into the woods.

Kate came through the trees. "Bailey! I was so afraid for you." She hugged her friend. "Are you all right?"

"I'm fine. But my legs felt like noodles for a minute there."

Biscuit scampered up to Bailey and jumped to get her attention.

"I see you! Thanks for scaring that elk away. You really

are a wonder dog!" She gave the dog a friendly rub. "But you scared us when you ran off into the woods!" Bailey slipped her lip balm from her pocket and applied some. "Now all we have to do is find the trail."

"Shouldn't be too hard with this GPS."

"Let's see that thing." Kate placed the tiny device in Bailey's palm. "I've never seen one this small."

"Dad says it still has a few glitches, but it works well for the most part." Kate took the GPS back. "See? It shows where we are. It looks like this squiggly line might be a trail."

"So we need to turn around and go to our right to find it. Let's try it."

Kate started off in the direction the GPS indicated. Bailey and Biscuit followed close behind. She kept her eye on the device and could see the distance between them and the trail diminishing. "We're almost there!"

"I think I see it!" Bailey went running, Biscuit barking excitedly beside her.

"I was thinking," Kate said when they were back on the trail. "I wonder if Justin and Joe know something about the elk being so agitated."

"Maybe. They sure are angry themselves."

"Maybe Justin is giving anger lessons to the elk."

Seeing the twinkle in Kate's eyes, Bailey laughed. "Yeah, they were probably just waiting for their class to gather when we snuck up on them."

"They seem to spend a lot of time on this hill."

"Yeah. And with that 'walking stick' that looked just like the gun they were shooting pop cans with today."

Just then the ground trembled.

"Did you feel that?" Kate asked.

Before Bailey could answer, the trembling became stronger. "Don't tell me it's another—"

The girls heard loud rustling and soon Bailey spotted a herd of elk running through the forest toward them. "Stampede!"

Kate snatched up Biscuit, grabbed Bailey's arm, and pulled her behind a tree. About twenty elk thundered by so close Bailey thought she could stick out her hand and touch them as they passed. She saw what looked like fear in their eyes and heard their snorts and panting. When the last one was out of sight, the fading rhythm of hooves was all that remained, followed by an eerie quiet. Bailey and Kate cautiously stepped out from behind the protection of the tree and looked around. A cloud of dust marked the path the elk had taken.

"I hope they don't run clear into town." Kate's eyes registered her concern.

"Something back there in the woods scared them. Why else would they run like that?"

"I don't know, but I think you're right."

"Y–You don't think it was a wild animal, do you?" Bailey forced the words from her mouth, barely daring to speak them.

Kate turned to her friend, eyes wide. "Let's get out of here!"

The girls ran down the trail until they could see the town. "We're almost there," panted Bailey.

"Are you okay? Do you need your inhaler?"

Bailey shook her head. "I'm okay. Just winded."

They slowed down and walked the rest of the way to town. When they got on Main Street, they heard people talking about the elk.

"I can't believe they came through here again!"

"This is the worst it's ever been."

"What are we going to do about them?"

"The elk are becoming too dangerous."

"Something has to be done."

Bailey pulled Kate aside where no one would hear them. "Do you think we should tell them what happened on our hike?"

"You mean our encounter with the elk, the elk stampede, getting separated and lost, or seeing Justin and Joe target practicing?"

Bailey giggled. "I guess we did have a lot going on, didn't we? Should we tell any of it?"

"I'm not sure. It might not have anything to do with the stampede through town."

"Then again it might." Bailey let out a giant sigh. "Maybe we should just go back to the hotel."

"Yeah. We need to gather more evidence before we

point fingers at people."

"Let's take the shuttle back. I'm tired of walking."

"Me, too." Kate hooked Biscuit's leash on him and set him down. "It's a wonder you didn't get trampled by that huge elk or the stampeding herd," she said in his pointy little ear. "You are so brave!"

"It's amazing none of us did," Bailey added. "God must be working overtime keeping an eye out for us."

"As usual."

The girls joined a couple of people who were waiting at the shuttle stop.

Kate plopped down on the bench. "We should get in touch with the other Camp Club Girls when we get back."

"Yeah, they'll want to hear about our adventure."

A voice interrupted their conversation, and Justin and Joe's grandma joined them under the shelter. "Oh, hi girls!"

"Mrs. Perkins! What are you doing here?"

"I've been doing a little shopping this morning." She held up her bags as proof. The shuttle pulled to the curb and the group boarded. Bailey and Kate sat across the aisle from Grandma Perkins and her shopping bags. Biscuit sniffed them curiously.

"What have you girls been up to?" Grandma Perkins asked.

"We went for a hike this morning and now we're heading back to the hotel."

"Justin and Joe were hiking today, too!"

Bailey bit her lower lip. "Yes, we saw them."

"My stomach is growling." Kate put her hand on her tummy.

Bailey, relieved at the change of subject, looked at her watch. "That's because it's lunchtime. It's almost twelve o'clock."

"Guess we timed that right."

When the shuttle parked in front of the hotel, Bailey, Kate, Biscuit, and Grandma Perkins got off.

"Oh, Mrs. Perkins! Did Mr. Perkins win the bugling contest?" Kate asked.

"No, someone else won," Grandma Perkins replied.

Bailey could hardly believe her ears. "That's impossible! He was the best one there!"

"Well, I'm glad you thought so, but the judges didn't agree." Grandma Perkins's voice was kind. "It's all right. He just did it for fun. He didn't care if he won."

"I bet Justin and Joe were really disappointed," Bailey said quietly as they walked down the hotel sidewalk.

"Yes, they were." Mrs. Perkins shook her head. "Especially Justin."

Bailey suddenly stopped and gasped.

"What's the matter?" Kate's eyes followed Bailey's line of vision toward the old historic building.

"I thought I saw a ghost in that window."

"Bailey! You know better than that!" Kate laughed but then paused. "You're as white as a sheet!"

"Which window?" Grandma Perkins asked.

"The fourth floor, four windows over from the right."

"Ah, yes. The famous room 408. And what did this ghost look like?"

"Like a cowboy. He had a cowboy hat and a mustache and he just stared out the window then faded off to the left."

"That must be the old cowboy ghost we read about in the brochure!" Kate kept her eyes on the window.

"Legend has it that a guest thought he saw the same thing years back," Grandma Perkins explained. "But the front desk confirmed that the room was vacant. They said no one could have stood in that window because it was over the bathroom sink, and he couldn't have faded to the left because it would have taken him through the wall. That was the first reported sighting of the cowboy ghost. Many people have seen him since then, but only at this time of the year."

"Are you telling me I saw a real ghost?" Bailey's voice trembled.

"Bailey! You're not going to fall for that, are you?"

"All I'm saying is that you're not the first to have seen it—whatever it is." Grandma Perkins patted Bailey on the back. "You want me to walk you to your room?"

"That's okay. We don't believe in ghosts, do we, Bailey?"

"N–no. We don't."

"Okay, then. I'll see you later." Mrs. Perkins left with a friendly wave.

Bailey and Kate stood in the hotel yard, still trying to absorb what had just happened.

"Do you believe that? I mean, really. Who would believe in cowboy ghosts?" Kate snickered as she looked up at the fourth floor window again.

Bailey stood silent beside her, but then she noticed Kate's face grow pale. Bailey followed Kate's eyes and this time they both saw the cowboy. "There he is! I told you it was real!" Bailey's voice quivered.

Kate reached for Bailey's hand. Her mouth moved, but no words came.

Now it was Bailey's turn to reassure Kate. "It has to be special effects, don't you think, Kate? Remember, there are no such things as ghosts."

No sooner had she said those words than the cowboy faded away to the left of the window just as he had done before.

"That is definitely a special effect. It's identical to the movement I saw before!" Bailey squeezed Kate's hand. "Come on. We've got another mystery to figure out. Hopefully, it will be as easy as finding out where the ghost children's laughter came from."

Kate nodded mutely as Bailey led her to the hotel entrance.

Mystery Music

Back in the hotel room, Bailey and Kate bathed Biscuit in the sink. Water sprayed everywhere when he shook himself. The girls screamed with laughter and wrapped the dog in a hotel towel.

"There you go!" Kate dried him off. "Nice and clean."

While the girls fixed sandwiches from food the Changs had put in the mini-fridge, they told Mrs. Chang about their hike and the beautiful scenery. They left out the parts about Justin and Joe, getting lost, and how close they were to the elk stampede.

"When we got back to town, the elk had just stampeded again and everyone was talking about it," Bailey told her.

"Oh no! Not again." Mrs. Chang shook her head. "Was anyone hurt?"

"I don't think so." Kate's green eyes were serious behind her dark-rimmed glasses. "They say it's the worst it's ever been and that they're going to have to do something about it because it's getting too dangerous."

Mrs. Chang nodded as she straightened up their room.

"I can believe that. They can't just let the elk run wild in town."

Bailey plugged in the charger for her laptop. "I still think there has to be a reason they're acting so crazy this year. We just have to uncover it."

"Sounds like you had a nice morning, in spite of the stampede," Mrs. Chang said.

"We did!" Bailey replied enthusiastically. "Grandma Perkins rode home on the shuttle with us."

"And when we got to the hotel, we saw the cowboy ghost of room 408!" Kate squealed.

"Cowboy ghost?" Mrs. Chang got that you've-got-to-be-kidding-me look on her face.

Bailey nodded. "We know he's not real, Mom. We just want to figure out how they do the special effect."

"Yeah, like the ghost children. We figured *that* one out." Kate reached for her laptop.

"Well, I guess there's no harm in that." Mrs. Chang glanced at her watch. "Oh, it's time for me to pick up Trina. She and a girl she met here at the hotel went to a movie. Will you be all right for a little while?"

"Yeah. We're going to get online and chat with the other Camp Club Girls."

"Okay. See you later." Mrs. Chang dropped a kiss on Bailey's nose and left.

"Let's download the pictures we took to send the other girls before we chat with them," Kate suggested. "Then they'll have them to look at while we talk."

Bailey and Kate each downloaded their photos and then logged into the CCG Web site chat room.

Bailey: *Hi! Anybody there?*

McKenzie: *I'm here.*

Sydney: *Me, too.*

Kate: *Hang on. I'll call the others to get them to log on.*

Elizabeth: *I'm here now.*

Alex: *Me, too.*

Bailey: *We found something weird on the hike we went on this morning.*

Elizabeth: *What was it?*

Kate: *We don't know. But we're hoping some of you might help us figure it out. We sent you some pictures of it.*

Bailey: *We hiked up a trail and found this weird, huge indentation in the ground. It was about the size of a bathtub. It had what looked like elk hair and tracks around it and it smelled awful. Sydney, we were hoping you could tell us if the tracks look like they belong to an elk. You'll see them in the pictures, too.*

Sydney: *I'll look and see. And I bet I know what that indentation was, too.*

Kate: *What?*

Sydney: *Hang on. I'll look at the picture to be*

sure. There it is. Yep. Was there any water nearby?

Bailey: *Yeah, we saw a scummy pond with grass growing in it a few feet away.*

Sydney: *It was probably an elk wallow. And those are definitely elk tracks in the picture. My uncle hunts elk and he told me about them. Usually the male elk, the bulls, roll in wallows to cover their bodies with the scent of urine and droppings so they'll attract the female elk.*

Elizabeth: *Gross! What nasty cologne!*

Sydney: *You think that's bad? The female elk then roll in the wallow to get the same scent on them and let the bull know they're interested.*

Alex: *I'd rather pass notes.*

Sydney: *One thing's for sure. If you have wallows, you have elk.*

Bailey: *Anyway, back to the hike. We caught Justin and Joe shooting airsoft guns at some empty pop cans. We sent you a few shots of that, too, no pun intended! Just look at the pictures. They're a little blurry. The noise from the gun scared Biscuit to death!*

Kate: *Yeah, he flew out of my arms and ran at them, barking his head off.*

Bailey: *Justin, or should I say Oscar the Grouch,*

*was so scared he aimed his gun right at poor
little Biscuit and shot!*

McKenzie: *Oh no! Is he okay?*

Kate: *Yeah, he wasn't hurt. Apparently our
wonder dog is faster than a speeding bullet or
else Oscar the Grouch is a lousy shot. Biscuit
must have just been freaked out over the
sound of the gun because he ran into the
woods and I ran after him.*

Bailey: *And I stayed to give those boys a piece of
my mind!*

Sydney: *LOL. Careful. You might need that piece
of your mind later.*

Elizabeth: *Guess you forgot the Bible says, "A
gentle answer turns away wrath, but a harsh
word stirs up anger."*

Bailey giggled.

Bailey: *Guess I did.*

Kate: *I found Biscuit after calling for him awhile.
But then I realized I had wandered off the
path and didn't know how to get back.*

Bailey: *In the meantime, I had gone to find Kate
and Biscuit and I realized I was lost, too. But
I asked God to help me. Then He gave me the
idea to call Kate on her cell.*

Kate: *Boy, was I glad to hear from her. We
remembered what Sydney taught us about*

using the position of the sun to figure out what direction we needed to go.

Sydney: *Wow! I'm impressed!*

Kate: *So when we got back together, we used my dad's mini-GPS I had in my pocket to find the trail so we could get back to the town.*

Sydney: *Wait a minute. Back up. What do you mean "caught" the boys shooting their airsoft gun at the pop cans? They weren't really doing anything wrong.*

Bailey: *No, but they sure acted like they got caught at something.*

Kate: *They were defensive and angry.*

Elizabeth: *Maybe they didn't like being spied on.*

Kate: *Or maybe they're up to no good since they act that way no matter when we see them or what they're doing.*

Bailey: *Wait! I just remembered something I heard Justin say to Joe before he knew we were there. He said something like "We'll make them sorry they ever came here."*

McKenzie: *Who do you think they were talking about?*

Bailey suddenly felt like a rock dropped to the bottom of her stomach.

Bailey: *I hope he wasn't talking about Kate and me, but he sure seems to hate us.*

Kate: *But why?*

McKenzie: *You must be a threat to them in some way.*

Bailey: *How can we be a threat to them when they don't even know us?*

McKenzie: *They're obviously insecure. You just have to figure out why.*

For just a second, Bailey felt sorry for the boys, especially Justin. She remembered her mom saying maybe they had problems at home or something. Maybe they just needed someone to care about them. Bailey's loud sigh drew Kate's eyes from her computer.

Bailey: *Maybe we just need to keep being nice to them. Find out what they're interested in and stuff like that. They could be going through a rough time or something and that's what makes them so grouchy.*

Elizabeth: *That's a good idea. I'm proud of you, Bailey.*

Bailey: *I'm not saying it'll be easy. But I'll try.*

Kate: *Guess what?*

Alex: *I'll bite. What?*

Kate: *Bailey and I saw a new ghost at the hotel today.*

Sydney: *No way!*

Bailey: *Room 408. The room with the cowboy ghost.*

Kate: *Of course it has to be another special effect. It moves exactly the same every time it's seen. We're going to figure out how they do it.*

Bailey: *Yeah. He shows up in the window and stares out a minute then fades away to the left. The only problem is that if he was a real person, he'd plow into a wall if he turned that way.*

Alex: *Didn't they use some sort of projection system to make it look like there were ghosts in the movie* Casper? *They could be using one in that room, too. Or once I saw a movie where an image was etched onto a window and the sun shining on it made it come to life. Maybe you should look more closely at the window.*

Kate: *We'll do that. Bailey and I need to take a tour of that room to see if we spot anything unusual. Anyway, we just wanted to update you. Let us know if you have any more ideas about how ghosts could be created or any new information about elk.*

Bailey logged off and closed her laptop.

"All right." Kate exited the chat room and brought up

a blank document. "Let's see what we have so far in the elk mystery. One. We know the elk are spooked but don't know why." She typed the entry into the blank document.

Bailey jumped in. "Two. We know Justin and Joe have an airsoft gun and were in the woods today before the stampede."

Kate typed the second entry. "But then again, so were we."

"Three. Justin has a grouchy attitude all the time."

"Four. They visit their grandparents here every year." Kate continued typing but stopped. "We don't even know if any of this has anything to do with the elk problem."

"No, but a good sleuth follows hunches," Bailey said. "And I have a hunch it does."

"I hope we're not going down the wrong path." Kate looked thoughtful. "What about what we know about elk?"

"Well, we know they make wallows during mating season," Bailey offered.

"And we know they are more aggressive during that time as well."

"But not usually this much."

"We know they have a great sense of smell and can run really fast," Kate said as she typed.

"Boy, do we know that!" Bailey laughed. "We learned they're usually most active in the early morning and later in the evening, unless they're being harassed."

"That may be a key to this mystery."

"We know the male elk are the ones with that shrill bugle." Bailey did her best impersonation of an elk bugle, starting with the low grunts and ending with a high shriek.

Biscuit sat up and howled while Kate covered her ears and laughed. "You aren't quite ready for that bugling contest yet!"

"I still can't believe Grandpa Perkins didn't win that."

"I can't either. I wonder if that's why Justin was so grouchy today."

"Maybe. Something must be making him mad." Bailey felt a little sad inside, like when she knew a friend was going to do something wrong but she couldn't talk her out of it. She turned at the sound of the key card sliding in the door.

"Hey!" Mrs. Chang gave her standard greeting. "What are you two up to?"

"We just finished chatting with the other Camp Club Girls," Bailey said. "How was your movie, Trina?"

"Not bad." The teenager flipped on the TV.

"We told the other girls all about our hike and seeing the cowboy ghost," Kate told Mrs. Chang.

"Sounds like you had fun. By the way, Bailey, Dad and I are going out to a business dinner tonight."

"What about us?" Bailey stuck out her lower lip.

"Adults only, I'm afraid." Mom's eyes brightened. "But how about a pizza party? We can have it delivered to our room."

"Yeah!" Bailey and Kate gave each other a high five.

"How 'bout it, Trina?" Bailey asked.

"Fabulous." Trina said in a monotone, still channel surfing.

"It'll be fun!" Bailey informed her sister brightly.

"Whatever." Trina gave up on finding something to watch and turned off the TV. She flopped on the bed and started listening to her iPod.

"I'm going to get cleaned up and then I'll call in the pizza." Mrs. Chang headed for the shower.

A while later, Bailey whistled when her mom emerged looking fresh and pretty in her black dress, dangly earrings, and strappy heels. The familiar smell of her mom's perfume made Bailey want to snuggle in her lap like she did when she was a little girl.

"What kind of pizza do you want?"

"Pepperoni!" Bailey shouted.

"With black olives?" Kate asked.

"Sure, I like olives and so does Trina."

"Pepperoni and black olives it is." Mrs. Chang phoned in the order.

While they were waiting for the pizza, Mr. Chang came home and spruced up, too.

"You guys look great!" Bailey said.

A knock at the door signaled the beginning of the pizza party. Mr. Chang paid for the food and set it on the small table. Then he tapped Trina on the shoulder and she took out her earphones.

"We should be home between nine and ten," he told her.

"You're in charge while we're gone. You hear that, Bales?"

Bailey and Kate both nodded.

The Changs blew the girls a kiss good-bye and told them to call on the cell phone if anything came up.

"We can handle this, Mom," Trina said.

"Good. I know you can. Have fun."

As soon as the door closed, the trio playfully shoved their way to the pizza. Trina lifted the lid. "Mmmm. Smell that."

They each took a slice and chatted and giggled as they ate. Kate fed Biscuit a couple of pieces of pepperoni.

"Trina, did you leave your iPod on?" Bailey asked.

"No. Why?"

Bailey cocked her head to listen. "I thought I heard piano music."

Trina put one earphone in. "Nope. It's not this."

"Listen. There it is again." Bailey craned her neck forward.

"I hear it, too." Kate said. "It's very soft, though."

"Sounds like old-fashioned music to me." Bailey went to the window to see if anyone was playing music outside but saw only people quietly strolling in the courtyard.

The music became louder.

"I hear it now." Trina joined Bailey at the window.

"It's not coming from outside." Kate put her ear to the air vent on the floor. "It sounds like it's coming through the vent!"

"It sounds. . .spooky." Kate shivered.

"Let's just turn on the TV and forget about it," Trina suggested.

The girls all sprawled out on the beds as Trina flipped through the channels.

A romantic comedy came on. "Oooo. This looks good." Trina fluffed her pillow and put it behind her back against the headboard.

"Didn't our hotel brochure say that F. O. Stanley's wife played the piano and sometimes guests still hear her music?"

"I think you're right! But would we be able to hear it clear up here?"

The eerie music continued.

Finally Bailey couldn't stand it anymore. "I don't know, but I'm going to find out where that music is coming from!"

"I'll come with you!" Kate announced.

"Fine with me," Trina said, still glazed over by the TV. "Just don't leave the building."

"Deal." Bailey grabbed another slice of pizza to munch on while they investigated.

Grabbing Biscuit, they walked down the hallway. The music seemed to get louder. Reaching the elevator, they pressed the DOWN button. When they reached the hotel lobby, the music was much louder.

Bailey marched to the front desk. "Excuse me."

Barbara, the surly hotel clerk, scowled at Biscuit.

"Can you tell me where that music is coming from?" Bailey smiled sweetly.

"From the Music Room, to your right." Barbara pointed to the room at the end of the lobby.

"The Music Room. Of course. Thank you." With a polite nod, Bailey turned to leave.

"And keep that dog under control."

"I will." Kate gave the woman a thumbs-up and raised Biscuit's paw in a wave.

Bailey and Kate walked on the lobby's shiny wooden floor to the doorway of the Music Room, the piano music growing ever louder. Stopping at the door, they peeked inside and saw that the room was unfurnished except for a grand piano at the far end. It sat in a raised alcove, almost a small, rounded room in itself. Its lid was propped open to allow the beautiful music to flow unhindered. A huge fireplace with white columns upholding the mantel took up most of the left wall. A giant mirror hung above it. Arched windows lined the other walls, with square-paned ones in the piano alcove. The piano sat sideways, but Bailey could clearly see the keys moving up and down from the door, though no one appeared to be playing it.

Bailey swallowed hard and looked at Kate, who had just used her free hand to remove her glasses and rub her eyes. She put them back on, steadying herself against the door frame. She and Bailey nodded pale-faced at each other. A ghost!

Trampled!

Kate, carrying Biscuit, followed Bailey cautiously across the threshold onto the glossy-wood Music Room floor. Immediately, the music stopped. Bailey grabbed Kate's arm. They tiptoed toward the piano, as if they were sneaking up on the ghost.

"Maybe whoever was playing will appear," Bailey whispered.

"I doubt it. But maybe we'll be able to see how they're doing the special effect."

"Yeah. I have to keep reminding myself it isn't real."

The girls stepped up into the alcove and inspected the piano.

"I wish I'd brought Biscuit's leash." Kate shifted the dog to her other arm and looked closer. "Aha! Just as I thought. It's a player piano."

"Huh?"

"A player piano. You know, the kind that has songs programmed into it so it plays by itself."

"Oh, I've seen those in stores. But doesn't someone have

to start and stop it?"

"Usually." Kate continued checking all angles of the piano. She wrestled with Biscuit who was getting wiggly. "I bet this one has an automatic switch or sensor somewhere that turns it on and off."

Bailey helped her search for a switch, even crawling underneath for a look. "I don't see anything."

Kate studied the strings and hammers for each key inside the piano. "There's so much stuff in here it's hard to tell what doesn't belong. But I think I may see something. Come over on this side for a better look."

Bailey was next to her in a flash.

"See that switch close to the hinge where the piano lid opens?"

"Yeah, I see it."

"I think it may be the culprit. And I think that box next to it is a timer that makes the music play only every so often."

"But how does it stop when someone comes in the room?"

Kate cocked her head and squinted her eyes. Bailey could practically see the wheels turning in her brain. "Maybe a motion sensor that's set to turn it off when someone comes through the door?"

"But we have to find it to be sure." Bailey's eyes started scanning the room. "There!"

Kate followed Bailey's finger to a small device mounted in the ceiling corner of the room. It was pointed directly at the doorway. "Yep, I bet that's our motion sensor."

"Let's go back out to the lobby and try it out." Bailey and Kate walked out to the lobby. They passed the time by looking at the Stanley Steamer car as they waited for the music to begin again.

Soon the melodious sound of the piano wafted into the lobby.

"There it goes!" Bailey made a beeline for the Music Room and stopped abruptly outside the door.

"Okay. Ready?"

"Ready." Kate grabbed Bailey's hand and together they walked into the room. The music stopped. "I'm sure the motion detector saw us."

"I wonder how sensitive it is," Bailey said. "Like, I mean, do we have to enter the room or just move in the doorway?"

"Interesting. Let's find out." Kate, Biscuit, and Bailey filed back out to the lobby so the piano could reset.

Soon the music began again.

"Let's go!"

Bailey and Kate stopped in front of the doorway. "Let's try just kicking our foot through the doorway, but not actually going in," Bailey suggested.

Kate giggled and locked arms with Bailey in chorus line fashion. "Okay. On three. One. . .two. . .three!"

Kate and Bailey each kicked one foot out. Once again, the music stopped.

"Wow! Pretty sensitive!" Bailey grinned from ear to ear.

"Guess we've pretty much solved this mystery. Might as well go back to the room."

"Hey, there goes Justin and Joe across the yard." Bailey pointed toward the window. The floodlights shining on the yard spotlighted the two boys as they walked away from the hotel. One turned around as if to see if anyone was following them.

"Is that their gun he's carrying?" Kate asked.

"Couldn't be. It's too dark for target practice."

"Weird."

The boys disappeared into the shadows.

"Know what I was thinking?" Bailey asked.

"What?"

"I wonder if anyone's staying in room 408."

Kate headed for the front desk. "We could check. And if no one is, we could ask if we can go see it tomorrow."

"Exactly what I was thinking." Bailey asked Front Desk Barbara if the room was vacant.

"Hmmm. Let me check." Barbara typed something into her computer and waited. She ran her finger down the screen until she came to the line she wanted. "Yep. Looks like it's vacant."

"Can we go look at it tomorrow?" Kate asked.

"What for?"

"We're curious about Tex." Bailey smiled knowingly at Kate.

"Tex?" Barbara smirked.

"Yeah. You know. The cowboy ghost. We think we saw him this afternoon from the front lawn."

"Well, I'm off tomorrow, so you'll have to check back with whoever's working then."

"Okay. Thanks." Kate gave a friendly wave as they walked off.

Bailey let out a laugh. "I just had a crazy idea."

"Oh no. What?"

"Let's see if Justin and Joe want to see the room with us tomorrow."

"No way!"

Bailey put her hand out. "Aw, come on. We just talked to the other girls today about trying to get to know them better. What if they really are going through something bad and just need a friend?"

"I seriously doubt that."

"Well, so do I. But what's the harm in asking them? They'll probably just say no anyway."

"That's true. All right. Let's do it."

Suddenly, a man burst through the front door of the lobby. "The elk! They're stampeding again, and this time someone's hurt!"

Bailey and Kate hurried outside. Elk ran frantically in front of the hotel, sending some of the guests scrambling for cover on the porch. Biscuit leaped out of Kate's arms and darted right into the herd.

"Biscuit!" Kate screamed. The dust settled from the

stampede, and people ran in all directions. Kate and Bailey sprinted to the yard where Biscuit lay motionless.

Kneeling beside the little dog, Bailey saw blood pooling beneath his right front paw. Ragged breaths puffed from his open mouth, and his tongue hung out one side. His eyes were open, but he didn't appear to see anything. "Oh, Biscuit!" Kate cried.

Shivering from the cold, Bailey pulled her cell phone from her pocket and steadied her finger to dial.

"Hello?" Trina said.

"Trina! The elk stampeded and Biscuit got trampled." Bailey choked down a sob. "We're on the front lawn. We need help."

"I'll be there as soon as I call Mom and Dad."

Bailey returned her phone to her pocket and wrapped her arms around herself to ward off the night chill.

Kate gently stroked the injured dog's side. "Hang on, Biscuit. Help's coming."

Bailey heard a siren in the distance. "Sounds like help is on its way for the people who were injured. I don't know if they'll help dogs, too, or not."

Within minutes, a red and white ambulance screeched to a halt at the far side of the lawn where a group of people gathered. Medics knelt on the ground next to their patient, then lifted him onto a stretcher and loaded him through the open back doors of the vehicle. Just as Bailey and Kate turned their attention back to Biscuit, they heard another siren. Looking back, they saw a second, and then a third ambulance arrive and take away two more people. Police cars began to filter in also, as well as news reporters.

"Those elk must have really been mad to run right into all those people," Bailey said sadly. "Or scared out of their wits."

"I hope the people who got hurt will be all right." Kate's forehead wrinkled with concern.

"We need to pray for them tonight—and Biscuit."

"Bailey!" Trina ran to them from the porch, carrying sweatshirts for both girls. "Thought you might need these."

"Thanks." Bailey slipped into her hoodie. "Biscuit's hurt bad. We don't know if we should move him or not. We don't want to injure him any more than he already is."

"That was smart of you." Trina put her arm around Kate, who wiped her eyes and nose with the sleeve of her sweatshirt. "I called Mom and Dad," Trina told her. "They heard about the stampede at the restaurant and were on their way home before I called. They'll know what to do."

"I think we need to say a prayer right now for Biscuit." Bailey laid her hand on the injured dog.

Trina took Kate's left hand, leaving her right hand free to continue comforting her dog.

"God, we're scared for Biscuit. Help him to be strong and brave. Help Mom and Dad to get here fast so it's not too late." Bailey's voice broke. She cleared her throat and went on. "Heal whatever is wrong with Biscuit. Help him to be good as new again, fast. Be with Kate. Give her comfort and peace. And help the people who got hurt tonight to be okay. Thank You for being here with us. Amen."

"Thanks, Bailey." Kate hugged her friend. "I just know Biscuit is going to be all right. He has to be."

"Girls!" Mr. and Mrs. Chang rushed up and hugged them. "We came as quickly as we could."

Mr. Chang looked at Biscuit. "I'll take Biscuit to the car so we can get him to the animal hospital. I parked right over there. Trina, you run ahead and open the door." He tossed her the keys.

"Where is the nearest animal hospital?" Bailey asked.

"A man at our dinner tonight recommended a vet that's not too far from here." Mr. Chang gently lifted Biscuit.

"Guess God worked that out for us, huh?" Kate said quietly as she followed Mr. Chang to the car.

"God's like that." Mrs. Chang smiled at Kate then put her arm around her and pulled her into a hug.

●—●—●

The animal hospital wasn't busy, and Biscuit was taken right in. The vet examined him and found he had a few broken ribs and a crushed paw. Wrapping the paw in a neon green bandage with dog bones printed on it, he explained, "I'm going to give Biscuit an injection of pain medicine. It will help him sleep comfortably for a while so he'll have some time to heal. I'll also wrap his body to keep him from moving too much. We don't want those broken ribs to puncture a lung."

Kate asked, lips trembling, "Can we take him home now?"

"We'll need to keep him overnight for observation, but if all goes well, he should be released tomorrow."

Bailey heard Kate sigh with relief. Biscuit was going to be okay!

●—●—●

"So you heard about the stampede, but we didn't get to tell you about the ghosts yet!" Bailey told her family on the way back to the hotel.

"Not again," Trina moaned and dramatically threw her arm over her eyes.

"Well, not real ghosts, of course, but we figured out the secret of how they make them seem real."

Bailey and Kate told the family all about the Music Room and the mysterious piano playing.

"Pretty good!" Trina said when they were finished with their elaborate, don't-leave-out-a-detail explanation.

"And tomorrow, we're going to see if we can get permission to see room 408 to try and learn the tricks they're using to make the cowboy ghost." Bailey rubbed her hands in anticipation.

"We'll have to see how that works out since we need to pick up Biscuit tomorrow," Kate reminded her. "I might need to stay with him."

"That's okay. I won't go without you."

"Or you could just go with Justin and Joe." Kate gave Bailey a playful nudge.

"Like that would ever happen."

Mrs. Chang looked toward the backseat. "What's this about the Perkins boys?"

"We thought we'd see if Justin and Joe wanted to see the haunted room 408 with us. But we figure they'll say no." Bailey felt her face get warm.

"Well, that was nice of you to think of them. I think those boys need some good friends like you." Mrs. Chang reached back between the front seats and patted Bailey's knee.

Mr. Chang pulled into a parking space in front of the hotel. "It's been quite a night. You girls handled the events of the evening very well."

Bailey pulled her hoodie closer around her and huddled against the cold night air as the group hustled into the hotel lobby. Mr. Chang walked directly to the front desk, Bailey and Kate close behind, while Mrs. Chang and Trina waited by the elevator.

"Do you have any information about the condition of the people who were injured in the stampede this evening?" he asked Front Desk Barbara.

"Only what the news has been reporting." Barbara pointed to the small TV in the corner of the reception desk. "They say three people were taken to the hospital. A man is in serious condition and the other two were treated and released."

"Something is going to have to be done to make sure this doesn't happen again."

"I heard the news reporter saying there's talk of putting up a fence along the wooded areas at the base of the hills to try to keep the elk from coming into town so easily."

Mr. Chang nodded and turned to leave. "Thanks for the information."

"What'd she say?" Trina asked when Mr. Chang joined them at the elevator.

The elevator dinged and the doors opened for them to get on. Bailey pushed the button for the fourth floor.

"Three people were hurt, but only one is still in the hospital. He's in serious condition."

"Wonder who it was." Bailey felt the elevator whisk them up to their floor.

The doors opened on the fourth floor and there stood Grandma Perkins.

"Mrs. Perkins! Good to see you again," Mr. Chang said.

"It's nice to see you, too." Grandma Perkins seemed to be in a hurry to get on the elevator and leave. Bailey noticed her eyes looked teary.

"Is everything all right?" Mrs. Chang asked her.

Grandma Perkins shook her head and turned her eyes away. "It's Glen. He was hurt in the elk stampede tonight. We thought it would be fun to surprise our grandsons with their favorite ice cream before they went to bed. When we got out of the car and were walking across the lawn, the elk charged through. Glen pushed me out of the way, but he got trampled. He's still in the hospital." Tears brimmed in her eyes.

"Grandpa Perkins was one of the people who got hurt?" Bailey cried.

Grandma Perkins nodded and wiped her eyes.

"I'm so sorry to hear that," Mrs. Chang said. "We heard someone was seriously hurt, but we didn't know it was him. We'll be praying for his quick recovery."

"Thank you." The older woman had a faraway look. "I just wish we could figure out what's causing those elk to act like this."

"I hope they come up with a solution before anyone else gets hurt," Mr. Chang said.

"I'd better get home. I'm about worn out from being at the hospital and from all the stress. I got a few bumps and bruises myself. My son sent me home and promised he'd stay with Glen tonight. Janice offered to drive me home, but I told her I was fine."

Mrs. Chang took Grandma Perkins's hands in hers. "Of course. Please let us know if we can do anything to help you or your family."

"Thank you so much." She pushed the button and the doors closed.

●—●—●

"I can't believe it." Bailey shook her head as they entered their room. "Grandpa Perkins is such a nice man. I wish he hadn't gotten hurt."

"We have lots of things to pray about tonight, don't we?" Mrs. Chang said. "Including thanking God that none of us were injured. You girls were pretty close to the action. I'm glad you're all right." She kissed all three girls on the head.

"Mom, do you think we could go see Grandpa Perkins at the hospital tomorrow?" Bailey asked.

"That would be nice, if they let kids in. I'll have to check the hospital rules first. We wouldn't stay long. He needs his rest to get better."

"I feel sorry for Justin and Joe. They must be really sad." Kate pulled out her pajamas and headed for the bathroom to change.

Bailey's eyes met Kate's. She suddenly thought, *I hope they weren't responsible for that elk stampede!*

CHAPTER 10

The Cowboy Ghost

The next morning, through a fog of sleepiness, Bailey heard her dad leave for one of his meetings. She had an uneasy feeling but couldn't put her finger on what it was. Then it came to her—the stampede the night before. Biscuit was hurt and so was Grandpa Perkins. It seemed like a bad dream.

Kate rolled over and stretched. "Biscuit?" Still half-asleep, she felt around the bed for him.

"Kate, Biscuit's not here, remember?" Bailey whispered, not wanting to wake the others.

Kate sat up, worry lines creasing her forehead. She rubbed her eyes, blew her nose, and put on her glasses. Her shoulders slumped like she held the weight of the world on them. "Oh yeah. I forgot."

"I was thinking," Bailey said softly, looking to see if her mom and Trina were still asleep. "The elk stampeded shortly after we saw Justin and Joe walking toward the hills last night."

"I know. I thought the same thing."

"I think they've been shooting at the elk and making

them charge into town."

Kate thought on that a moment. "The elk are being harassed and it's making them more aggressive, just like Sydney said."

"I bet if Justin and Joe caused the stampede, they're sorry for it now that their grandpa got hurt."

"If it's them, I hope they've learned their lesson." Kate's eyes blazed fiercely.

"But why would they want to make the elk stampede in the first place? I don't get it."

"I don't know, either. I have a feeling there's a whole other piece of this mystery that we haven't begun to figure out yet."

"I'm starting to think they're really messed up. They seem to have a nice family, so I don't think that's the problem." Bailey propped herself up on her elbow.

"No, it must be something else. McKenzie mentioned that they might feel threatened in some way. Maybe we need to think about what it could be."

"I know," Bailey replied. "I wish there was some way she could talk to Justin and Joe. She's so good at figuring people out."

"Guess for now we'll just have to rely on her suggestions and figure it out ourselves."

"I think we need to pray for them," Bailey said. "And we need to ask God to show us if there's some way we can help them."

"Maybe if we invite them to see room 408 with us today, we'll have a chance to learn more about them." Kate put her hand over her mouth and sneezed, waking Trina and Mom. She smiled sheepishly. "Sorry."

"Good morning to you, too," Trina mumbled then buried her head under her pillow.

"Do you know when we can go get Biscuit?" Kate asked Mrs. Chang.

"I'll call to find out." She looked at the clock. "They're probably just opening." She picked up the vet's business card and dialed the number. "Yes, this is Dory Chang and I was wondering how our dog, Biscuit, is doing and when we might pick him up." Mrs. Chang covered the mouthpiece of the phone and whispered to Kate, "They're checking."

Kate nodded.

Mrs. Chang directed her attention back to the person on the phone. "Okay. Thank you. We'll see you later. Bye."

"What'd they say?" Bailey asked.

"They said Biscuit is doing fine and we can pick him up this afternoon. They need to change his bandage this morning and check his vital signs. If something doesn't check out, they'll give us a call. Otherwise, he's good to go."

"Good. I can't wait to have him back," Kate said, beaming.

"Let's get dressed so we can ask the front desk if we can see room 408 before we get Biscuit." Bailey hopped off the bed and grabbed some clothes.

"Good idea. You think the boys will want to come after

121

what happened last night?" Kate asked.

"Hard to say. But it could be a nice distraction for them." Bailey slipped into her jeans and T-shirt. "I'm ready."

"Wait just a minute, missy," Mrs. Chang said in her mom voice. "You need to eat something and brush your teeth and hair before you go anywhere."

"Aw, Mom. We have ghosts to chase down." Bailey smirked at her mom.

"Then you'll need all the energy you can get from breakfast. Have a seat." Mrs. Chang set the box of cereal in front of her daughter and grabbed a carton of milk from the mini-fridge.

Kate quickly dressed and joined Bailey at the table. "Did the vet say anything else about Biscuit?"

"No, I'm afraid not."

"I can't wait to see him."

"We should turn on the morning news to see if there are any new developments about the stampede." Mrs. Chang grabbed the remote and pushed POWER.

"Witnesses say they observed some young men with guns just before the stampede. . . ," the newscaster said.

Bailey froze, her spoon halfway between her open mouth and her bowl. Kate choked on the bite she'd just taken. Coughing, she snatched a napkin from the table.

"Are you okay?" Mrs. Chang asked her.

"Y–Yes. I'm fine."

Bailey glimpsed her friend's worried eyes. They finished

breakfast, brushed their teeth and hair, and were out the door to go see if Justin and Joe wanted to go ghost hunting with them. Kate grabbed a small pad of paper and a pen in case they needed to take notes.

"I can't believe our suspicions about Justin and Joe were on the news!" Bailey said as they walked down the hall.

"I hope they didn't do anything." Kate knocked on the Perkinses's door.

A moment later, Mrs. Perkins answered. Bailey told them why they were there.

"Well, how thoughtful. Just a minute, I'll ask them."

A moment later she returned. "Thank you, girls, for thinking of them, but with all that's happened, they think they'll pass this time. We're going to go to the hospital to see their grandpa later. He was hurt in the stampede last night."

"Yes, we heard. I'm sorry." Bailey shifted her weight from one foot to the other. "Mrs. Perkins, do you know if they'd let us see Grandpa Perkins if we went? If children are allowed in the hospital?"

"Yes, I saw children visiting other patients last night."

Kate brightened up. "That would be great. We'd like to go visit him."

"That would be lovely. I know he'll be glad to see you."

"Okay. Well, tell Justin and Joe hi and that we're sorry about their grandpa."

"I'll do that." Mrs. Perkins closed the door.

Standing on tiptoe a short time later, Bailey leaned against the tall front desk. "Excuse me. We were wondering if we could see room 408, please."

The man at the counter smiled. "Barbara told me some young gals might be coming to ask about that."

Bailey looked at Kate, eyebrows high with surprise.

"Let me see. Yes, it's vacant, though I can't let you in without an adult. Would you like me to get a bellhop to take you?"

"Yes, please!" Bailey could hardly contain her excitement. They were going to get to see the haunted room!

"And what are your names?" the front desk clerk asked.

"I'm Bailey Chang, and this is Kate Oliver."

"Very good. I'll get someone to take you up."

"Thank you."

"Now remember," Kate said, pulling Bailey aside while they waited for the bellhop. "We need to look for anything that could be used to make it look like the cowboy appears in the window then fades to the left."

"Got it." Bailey turned at the sound of footsteps. A young man Bailey guessed to be in his twenties approached them.

"You must be Bailey and Kate." He stuck out his hand and shook Bailey's hand first, then Kate's. "I'm Lance. Nice to meet you. So you're interested in the cowboy ghost of room 408, huh?" he asked as they walked to the elevator.

Kate nodded. "We saw him from the front yard yesterday."

"What time of day was it?" The elevator doors opened and they stepped in.

"Around noon. Why?"

"Seems like that's the time most people see him these days."

Kate looked at Bailey, who widened her eyes.

"Why do you suppose that is?" Bailey asked, fishing for more information.

"It has something to do with the lighting. You know, the sun being directly overhead and all."

"Interesting." Kate pulled her pen and paper from her pocket and jotted down the lighting clue. The elevator doors opened, and Lance led them down the hall to room 408. He slid his key card through the slot and they heard it unlock, the tiny green light flashing. "Here we are! I'll wait here by the door for you. Take your time looking around."

Bailey gazed at the room that looked remarkably like their own room down the hall. Nothing special or haunted about it.

Kate walked slowly around the room, inspecting every wall and corner. Bailey followed her as she went to the window over the bathroom sink. It overlooked the front yard where they'd been standing yesterday when they saw the ghost.

"If the ghost looked like it faded to the left from out there," she said to Bailey, "then it would have to move to the right from in here, since it faced the window." Sure enough, the bathroom wall was right there, making it impossible to move in that direction.

"Alex thought we should feel the glass, remember?" Bailey asked.

Kate leaned closer to the window and ran her fingers over the glass. "There are definitely scratches or etching or something. I can feel them." She moved her open hand along the window's surface.

Bailey felt it, too. "Maybe people tried to claw their way out of here to escape the ghosts!"

Kate laughed. "I doubt that. I think Alex may be right. It's some kind of etching."

"Sometimes they put etched glass or thick blocks of glass in bathroom windows so no one can see in." Bailey scratched her head. "But who could see in way up here on the fourth floor?"

"We did! Or we thought we saw the cowboy ghost, anyway."

"Let's go out on the lawn at noon again today so we can check it out. We'll see if we see that cowboy ghost again. Maybe Lance will even bring us back up here then so we can see what it looks like from the inside."

Kate high-fived Bailey. "Let's go ask him."

Lance was leaning against the door frame listening to his iPod. He snatched the earphones from his ears when he saw the girls. "All done?"

"For now," Bailey replied. "But we were wondering if

there's any chance you could bring us back up here around noon. We want to see what the room looks like at the time of day we saw the cowboy."

"If I'm not busy with any other guests, I'll be glad to."

"Great! Thanks!"

"I'll walk you back down to the lobby." Lance extended his arm to show the way.

"Oh, thank you," Kate said, "but we're going back to our room now. It's just down this hall. Thanks for letting us in."

"No problem. I'll try to meet you in the lobby around noon."

Bailey followed Kate to their room. "Why did you want to go back to our room? There's not much to do there."

"We need to tell the other girls what happened last night." Kate's eyes grew serious.

"Oh, yeah. I almost forgot they don't know about Biscuit or Grandpa Perkins yet."

"Or that we're pretty sure Justin and Joe were involved in the stampede and that the news talked about boys with guns going into the hills just before the stampede."

"We do have a lot to cover with them!" Bailey slid her key card in the door.

"We're back," Bailey announced when they entered the room.

"I was just getting ready to call you." Mrs. Chang bustled around tidying up and then grabbed her purse. "Trina and I are going shopping. Do you want to go?"

Bailey looked at Kate to see if she wanted to go. She detected the slight shake of her head. "No. I don't think so. We were just there yesterday when we went hiking."

"Okay. You'll be all right here?"

Bailey nodded. "We're going to call the Camp Club Girls to tell them about last night's stampede and that Biscuit got hurt."

Mrs. Chang kissed Bailey on the cheek. "Sounds good. We'll probably be back around one o'clock or so. There are sandwich makings in the fridge if you get hungry. We'll go get Biscuit after Trina and I get home."

"Okay. See you later. Have fun!"

Kate dialed Elizabeth then conferenced in all the other girls, including Bailey.

"Everyone there?" Each one confirmed they were there and could hear each other.

"Good. We have a lot to tell you about since yesterday," Bailey said.

"Really? How much could have happened in less than twenty-four hours?" Alex asked.

"A lot! We'll start at the beginning. We heard creepy ghost music last night and went to investigate," Kate began. "Legend says it's the ghost of F. O. Stanley's wife, Flora, playing the piano. Turns out the ghost music came from the Music Room where she always played, but it's really just a piano player on a timer. If anyone comes into the room when it's playing, the music stops."

128

Bailey picked up the story. "We discovered it's on a motion sensor that's tied into the timer. So if the detector senses motion in the doorway, it turns off the timer and player piano, stopping the music."

"Awesome! You guys are getting good at this!" Sydney exclaimed.

Bailey laughed. "But that's not all! While we were still in the lobby, there was another stampede in front of the hotel."

"I was carrying Biscuit because I'd forgotten his leash," Kate added. "He heard the noise and bolted from my arms and ran outside."

"No!" Alex said.

"We chased after him, but it was too late." Kate's voice shook as she relived the horrible evening. "He'd been trampled by the elk and was lying in the grass with a bloody paw."

"It was terrible!" Bailey wailed. "Poor Biscuit could hardly breathe he hurt so bad."

"What did you do?" Elizabeth asked.

"We had to take him to the hospital," Kate said.

"And get this," Bailey said. "Someone had just told my parents where the closest one was and which vet to ask for!"

"Wow," Elizabeth said. "That sounds like a real God-thing!"

"Totally." Kate cleared her throat. "And the hospital was pretty close, too!"

"You did the right thing by not picking Biscuit up to

comfort him," McKenzie said. "A loving touch is all anyone really needs as they wait for help in a time like that. So how is he now?"

"Well, the doctor checked him over," Kate told her. "He had a crushed paw and some broken ribs. They wrapped his paw up in a big bandage and gave him some pain medicine to make him sleep so he could heal easier. We had to leave him at the hospital overnight, but we're going to get him this afternoon." Kate grinned triumphantly.

Sydney sighed. "That's a relief."

"Give the puppy a hug for me when he gets home," Alex said.

"And an extra treat from me!" McKenzie added.

"I'm glad he's going to be okay," Elizabeth said. "I'll be sure to remember him in my prayers. You know, in Proverbs, the Bible tells us a righteous man cares for the needs of his animals. I'd say you've done exactly that."

"Thanks, Lizzy." Kate smiled shyly at Bailey.

"But that's not the worst of it!" Bailey continued. "Three people were hurt in that stampede, too!"

"Oh no!" Sydney cried.

"Here's the sad part—the one hurt the most was Justin and Joe's Grandpa Perkins." Bailey couldn't bring herself to call Justin "Oscar the Grouch" under the circumstances.

"That is sad," McKenzie said. "How are they taking it?"

"We don't really know." Bailey shrugged, even though the others couldn't see it through the phone.

"We haven't actually talked to them ourselves yet."

"But here's the creepy part," Bailey continued. "We saw Justin and Joe walking toward the hills the night of the stampede."

"And it was only a few minutes later that the stampede happened." Kate bit her lower lip.

"We think they had their gun with them even though it was way too dark for them to do any target practice."

"Not only that," Kate added, "the news station this morning reported that witnesses had seen two young men with guns before the stampede. So we weren't the only ones who noticed."

"Man," Sydney said. "Those boys are going to have some explaining to do."

"You're telling me." Bailey pulled her lip balm out of her pocket and smoothed some on.

"We want to try to get to know them better to see if we can help them in any way," Kate said.

"They must be really afraid and lonely right now. Not to mention sad about their grandpa," McKenzie added. "They really do need some good friends like you."

Bailey and Kate then briefly told the Camp Club Girls about their trip to room 408 that morning.

"So we're hoping to go back up to see it around noon," Kate said.

"And we want to look at that window from the lawn at that time to see if the cowboy ghost shows up."

"Keep us posted," Alex said. "That sounds like an awesome hotel!"

"We will!" Bailey said. "And in the meantime, we have to figure out what the boys are so angry about."

"Maybe you'll remember something they said that will give you a clue," McKenzie said.

"Yeah, we'll have to think back about our conversations with them," Kate agreed.

Someone knocked at Bailey and Kate's hotel door, ending the conference call. Bailey made sure the chain was latched on the door before opening it the three inches it allowed. She inhaled sharply when she saw who stood on the other side.

Confession

Kate came to the door and peered out over Bailey's head to see Justin and Joe.

"Justin! Joe! What are you doing here?" Bailey unhooked the chain and opened the door.

"W–We just wanted to see if you want to go to the hospital with our family." Justin inspected his black and red Nikes as he spoke. "My mom said you wanted to visit my grandpa."

"Yes, we do," Kate said. "We're sorry he was hurt."

"The only problem is that my parents aren't here for me to ask permission right now." Bailey frowned.

"Can you call them?" Joe asked.

"Yeah. Sure." Bailey was so surprised by this unexpected invitation she could hardly get her words out. "When are you leaving?"

"Later this afternoon," Justin replied. "We just wanted to give you a heads-up in case you wanted to come along."

"I'll call my mom right now." Bailey grabbed her phone from her pocket and speed-dialed. "Mom? Can we go with the Perkinses to the hospital later today to see their grandpa? Okay. That should work. Thanks. Love you, too."

"Well?" Justin asked.

"She said yes. She'll pick us up at the hospital when she and my sister are done shopping, and then we'll pick up Kate's dog from the vet. Plus, she also wants to see your grandpa."

"Why's your dog at the vet?" Joe asked.

"He got trampled in the stampede, too," Kate said.

"He did? Is he all right?" Justin seemed genuinely concerned about the little dog.

"He broke some ribs, and his paw got messed up." Kate grimaced. "He had to spend the night there, but he's getting out today."

"He might not be quite as fast as he was when he saw you in the hills yesterday," Bailey teased the boys.

"Thank goodness for that!" Justin cracked a shy smile, the first Bailey had ever seen on his face. It was a nice smile, she decided, looking at his straight white teeth. He was cute.

"Thanks for inviting us to go with you," Kate said.

"We'll knock on your door when we're ready to leave." Joe seemed more relaxed than Bailey remembered him being before, maybe because Justin wasn't so irritable.

"Wait!" Bailey called. "We're going to check out room 408 where the cowboy ghost is always seen today at noon. You wanna come?"

Justin looked at Joe and shrugged. "Sure."

"We're meeting the bellhop, Lance, in the lobby then if you want to meet us there, too."

"Okay, we'll see you in the lobby at twelve o'clock," Joe said.

"Great. See you then." Kate shut the door and latched the chain.

"Can you believe that?" Bailey exploded.

"They're like different people today!"

"Well, they can't help but be changed by what happened to their grandpa." Bailey shook her head. "But I never dreamed the change would be this dramatic."

"Let's tell the girls we're going so they can pray that we have an opportunity to share our faith with the boys," Kate suggested. "This could be just the chance we've been waiting for."

Bailey snatched her laptop from the bed, and Kate grabbed hers off the nightstand. "We'll just have to tell whoever's online since we don't have time to get everyone together before they pick us up." Bailey logged on.

> Bailey: *Anyone out there?*
> Elizabeth: *Hi! I'm here.*
> McKenzie: *Me, too.*
> Kate: *Of course, I'm here.*

Bailey looked from her computer to Kate and they traded grins.

Bailey: *You'll never guess who was just here.*

McKenzie: *The ghost of Christmas past?*

Kate: *LOL. No, but a very good guess considering where we are.*

Bailey: *It was Justin and Joe!*

McKenzie: *No way! What'd they want?*

Kate: *They invited us to go with them to the hospital to see their grandpa.*

Elizabeth: *That's a miracle!*

Bailey: *That's what we thought. And they were actually nice to us, not grouchy at all.*

Kate: *We told them about Biscuit getting hurt and Justin asked if he was going to be okay.*

Bailey: *And he smiled a really nice smile when I teased him.*

McKenzie: *LOL. You're funny.*

Kate: *Anyway, we wanted you to be praying for us.*

Bailey: *Those boys really need Jesus in their hearts so they'll be happier.*

McKenzie: *And they'll need good friends to support them if they were involved in the stampedes.*

Elizabeth: *You can show them God's unconditional love. I'll be praying.*

Kate: *Thanks. We knew we could count on you.*

Bailey: *Plus, we invited them to go with us to check out the cowboy ghost and they said yes!*

McKenzie: *You're kidding!*

Kate: *I know. We can hardly believe it.*

Bailey: *We have to eat before then, so we'd better go. But maybe you can get the word out to the other girls so they can pray, too.*

Elizabeth: *Okay. We'll try. But about these ghosts you're chasing—just remember that Hebrews 9:27 says that man is destined to die once, and after that to face judgment.*

Bailey: *What's that supposed to mean?*

Elizabeth: *It means ghosts aren't real. Once we die, we're dead. We don't come back to haunt people as ghosts.*

Kate: *We know they're not real, Elizabeth, but thanks for the reminder.*

Bailey: *Yeah, thanks. It's easy to get carried away with this stuff sometimes. We'll keep you posted. See ya.*

Bailey logged off and closed her laptop. Kate got out the bread and started making a peanut butter and jelly sandwich.

"Something Justin said at the Elkfest just came to me," Bailey said.

Kate spread the peanut butter on her bread. "What was it?"

"I think it may be what McKenzie was talking about when

she said the boys must feel threatened somehow. Remember how Justin was so mad when we said we hoped Grandpa Perkins would win the bugling contest?" Bailey grabbed the peanut butter jar. "He said something about how the tourists shouldn't be able to win and should just go home."

"I thought he was just kidding," Kate said around a bite of sandwich.

"So did I until I looked at him. He was mad and dead serious." Bailey finished making her sandwich and poured a glass of milk.

"That could be it, Bailey!"

"Justin and Joe used to visit their grandparents here before all the tourists started coming. Maybe Estes Park has changed so much from all the tourists that Justin wants them to leave."

"He could be angry that their quiet vacation spot is now crowded and busy." Kate took another bite. "I bet the tourists don't take care of the place like the locals, either."

"I know I've seen some of the tourists littering and leaving messes behind," Bailey said.

"That would explain why Justin didn't like us at first. If he feels threatened by tourists, he'd feel threatened by us since we're tourists!"

Bailey stopped eating. "Maybe he's using that gun to scare the elk into town so they'll scare the tourists away."

"But how did he always know where to find the elk?" Kate asked.

Bailey bit into her sandwich and thought a second. Then her eyes lit up. "Sydney said one thing's for sure. If you have wallows, you have elk."

"That's it!" Kate yelled. "The wallows! The boys are finding the elk by finding the wallows. Bailey, I think we may have just figured out our mystery."

"Now we just have to prove it."

"Come on, we have to get down to the lobby. It's almost noon!"

As they exited the elevator, they saw Lance waiting for them. The Perkins boys showed up moments later.

"Everyone ready to check out room 408?" Lance asked.

"Can we start by looking at it from the courtyard first to see if we can see the cowboy ghost?" Bailey asked.

"Sure," Lance said. "I'll wait here for you."

The foursome went to the front yard and looked up to the fourth floor window.

"There he is!" Kate pointed at the image.

"Cool!" Justin said. "I've never actually seen him before."

"We've always heard about this, but never saw it for ourselves!" Joe added.

"Okay, so we know he's showing up right now," Bailey said. "Let's go to the room to see if we can figure out how it's happening."

Lance escorted them to the fourth floor and unlocked the door. The room was bright, flooded with sunlight.

"Look at the etching on the glass now," Bailey said. "You

can see a lot more of it with the sun shining directly on it."

"Yeah," Kate agreed. "I can see the whole image of the cowboy now."

"Why couldn't we see it before?" Bailey asked Lance.

He smiled. "You were right about the etching on the glass. When the sunlight shines directly on it, you can see all of it. But some of the etching is done so lightly that it only shows up under bright light. That's why you couldn't see the whole image this morning."

"Look!" Joe said. "A shadow is starting to move across the window."

Bailey and Kate looked at each other, eyes wide. "That must be what makes it look like the cowboy's turning toward the wall before he disappears!"

"Exactly," Lance said. "You guys are pretty smart."

"But wait a minute," Kate said. "If it depends on the sunlight to make it appear, then wouldn't it show up at different times of day depending on the time of year? You know, with the rotation of the earth and all."

Lance laughed. "Now you're really thinking! And you're right. You just happen to be here when the sun shines on it around noon. Other times of the year it's earlier or later in the day." He leaned toward Bailey and said in a mock whisper, "That makes it more mysterious."

"Wow." Bailey walked to the window and ran her hand over the etching. "I can't believe we figured that out."

"Well, we might not have if it weren't for Alex's help

about the etchings," Kate reminded her.

Lance looked at his watch. "I'd better get back to work."

"Thanks for showing us all this and confirming our theory," Kate said as they all left the room.

Closing the door behind him, Lance said, "My pleasure!"

Bailey turned to the boys. "I think we'll go out on the porch for a while. If we're not in our room when you're ready to go to the hospital, you can find us down there."

Joe nodded. "Okay, see you this afternoon."

●——●——●

At the hospital, everyone grew quiet. They'd chatted all during the ride, but when they turned into the parking lot, Justin and Joe were back to their usual grouchy faces. Justin's eyebrows made a sharp V-shape over his eyes.

Bailey and Kate walked in silence with the boys' family. When they came to Grandpa Perkins's room, Bailey could hardly believe it was him in the bed. Tubes snaked from his arms and nose. His face was bruised and swollen. His silver hair stuck out in odd places and lay too flat in others.

Grandma Perkins was sitting in a chair by the bed but stood when they entered the room. She motioned for Justin and Joe's dad to take her seat. The others sat on chairs that were brought in and put around the room. Bailey and Kate sat on the far side of the room while Justin and Joe parked themselves close to the door. Their mother stood on one side of Grandpa's bed and Mr. Perkins, now in Grandma's chair, took his father's hand.

"Hi, Dad. We're all here—Janice, Justin, Joe, and even our friends, Bailey Chang and Kate Oliver from down the hall at our hotel. Remember? They cheered you on during the bugling contest at the Elkfest."

Grandpa Perkins's eyelids fluttered then opened slightly. A faint smile crossed his lips.

"You don't have to say anything, Dad. Save your strength for getting better."

Bailey heard a chair scrape and saw Justin leave the room, followed by Joe. She looked at Kate, wondering if they should go. Kate nodded and they went into the hallway where they found Justin and Joe arguing in loud whispers.

"We can't tell!" Justin snapped.

"We have to," Joe said. "They'll find out sooner or later and it would be better if they heard it from us."

"Justin? Joe?" Bailey said.

The brothers' heads jerked toward them in surprise, their eyes blazing.

"Look, we don't mean to intrude, but maybe we can help." Bailey walked closer to Justin and Joe.

"What do you know about anything?" Justin barked.

Kate spoke gently. "We know you seem to be in trouble and we'd like to help."

"No one can help us," Joe said, tears filling his eyes.

"That's not true. If we can't help, we know who can." Bailey's voice was strong and confident.

"But first you have to tell us the problem." Kate stood waiting for their reply.

The boys remained silent.

Justin drew in a deep breath and blew it out slowly. He eyed Joe, who nodded. Justin looked at Bailey and she noticed his chin quiver. Tears pooled in his eyes. "It's our fault. My fault, really. Joe tried to talk me out of it," he finally whispered.

"What's your fault?" Bailey thought she knew, but she figured it was important for Justin to say it himself.

"The stampede. All of them. And Grandpa's injuries."

"How is it your fault? What did you do?" Kate asked.

"We—I—scared the elk. I shot around them with my airsoft gun to spook them. I never shot directly at the elk. Only in the trees and bushes around them. Joe came along because I pressured him. He didn't want to be involved."

"Why did you want to scare the elk? Didn't you see how it made them stampede?"

"Yeah, I saw," Justin replied. "That was the point. I remember when Joe and I were little and we'd come here to visit my grandparents. This place was awesome. It was so beautiful. But over the years the tourists began coming and it started to change. They didn't care about taking care of this place since they'd be going home in a week or two. They acted like they owned the place just because they threw their money around in all these shops.

"The Elkfest used to be just for the locals," he continued,

"but now all these fancy tourists were joining it. It made me sick. I wanted Estes Park to be peaceful like it used to be. It was our special place with our grandparents until those tourists ruined it. So I hoped the elk would scare them away."

"How did you know where to find the elk? It seems like you always knew where they were."

"I just looked for a wallow and knew they'd be close by."

"Just as we thought," Bailey said.

"Where there are wallows, there are elk." Justin smiled, but his eyes were sad. "Wait a minute. You *knew* that? Did you know what we were doing, too?"

Bailey nodded. She turned to Justin and put her hand on his arm. "It's okay, Justin. We're still your friends. We'll explain later. But you need to tell your parents."

Justin shook his head. "I can't."

"Sure you can. We'll go with you," Kate said. "And God will give you the strength to do what you need to do."

"You talk about God like He's standing right here with us," Justin said.

Bailey laughed. "That's because He is!"

"I wish I had faith like that," Joe said.

"You can!" Kate assured him. "You just have to ask God for it. He loves to help people believe."

Justin shook his head. "Seems like God wouldn't want anything to do with someone like me."

"That's the cool thing about God," Kate said. "He's not

like people who only love popular, nice-looking people, or those who never mess up. He especially loves those who need help and who have done things they shouldn't."

"When you really think about it, that includes all of us." Bailey could hardly believe they were having this conversation. She knew the Camp Club Girls' prayers were giving her and Kate the courage to tell the boys about God.

Justin looked at them. "Maybe you're right." He looked toward the hospital room door. "I guess it's time to tell them."

Bailey and Kate followed Justin and Joe back into Grandpa Perkins's room.

"I—I have something I need to say," Justin began. "I owe you a huge apology. I don't know if you'll be able to forgive me."

"Forgive you for what?" Mrs. Perkins looked surprised.

"For causing all this trouble."

"This isn't your fault, son," Mr. Perkins said. "No one could have stopped those elk."

"That's where you're wrong." Justin told the story to his parents and grandparents. "So if I hadn't been so stupid and wanted everything the way it used to be, I wouldn't have shot at the trees and bushes around the elk to spook them and this never would have happened. Grandpa's hurt because of me, and I'm so sorry."

Mr. Perkins's forehead creased with worry, but his words were gentle. "I'm disappointed in what you did,

Justin. I always taught you to be responsible with guns and never to use them for harm. You used your airsoft gun inappropriately, and there will be consequences." Mr. Perkins put his arm around his son's shoulder. "But it takes a strong man to admit when he's wrong. I'm glad you told the truth."

"You know you could never do anything to make us stop loving you," his mother said. "Not even this."

"I know." Justin's face relaxed. "You guys are the best."

Mr. Perkins turned to his younger son. "And Joe. I'm proud of you for not taking part in this. Even though you went with him, you did try to talk him out of it."

Joe ran to his father's arms and hugged him.

"However," Mr. Perkins added, "even if you couldn't stop Justin, you should have come to Mom or me. You should always speak up and tell an adult if you know someone is involved in dangerous activities. Maybe none of this would have happened." Justin's face was white, and Joe's ears went red. "You will both have consequences."

A tap at the door shifted their attention in that direction. "Hello?"

"Mom!" Bailey cried, glad to have the tension broken.

Mrs. Chang and Trina entered.

"How is he doing?" she asked.

"The doctor says he's making progress," Mr. Perkins said. "His vital signs are good. It's just a matter of time and healing now."

"He certainly is in our prayers," Mrs. Chang said.

"We appreciate that," Mrs. Perkins replied.

Mrs. Chang turned to the girls. "Kate, are you ready to go get Biscuit?"

"I'm more than ready!" Kate replied. "I can't wait to see him."

"Where is that cute little dog?" Mrs. Perkins asked. "On a playdate?"

"Oh no," Kate said seriously. "He's at the animal hospital. He was hurt in the stampede."

"No!" Mrs. Perkins went to Kate and took her hands in hers. "You were kind to come see Grandpa Perkins when Biscuit had an injury to be concerned about. I'm sorry I didn't know about it sooner."

"At least Biscuit is recuperating." Kate looked at Grandpa Perkins. "I wish Grandpa could go home today, too."

"He'll be home before we know it," Grandma Perkins piped in. "And stirring up trouble, no doubt."

"We'd better go," Mrs. Chang said. "You girls ready?"

"Yeah," Bailey said. Then turning to Justin and Joe, she said, "We'll be around if you want to talk or anything."

Justin smiled. "Thanks. We just might."

●—●—●

On the way to the vet, Bailey and Kate told Mrs. Chang and Trina what they'd learned.

"You're kidding!" Mrs. Chang said.

"Nope. And here's the cool part," Bailey said. "We got a chance to tell them about God and how He loves them no matter what they've done." Bailey's smile was as big as a watermelon slice.

"That is cool," Trina said.

"What did they say?" Mrs. Chang asked.

"Joe said he always wanted to have faith like that," Bailey said.

"And I told him God would help him believe if he just asked Him."

"You girls amaze me." Mrs. Chang looked at them in her rearview mirror. "I'm proud of you. And I bet God's smiling pretty big right now, too."

"I hope so," Bailey said. "We told them we would be around if they wanted to talk or anything."

"You've done what you can for now," Mrs. Chang said. "Now God will do His part and help them sort it all out." She pulled the car into a parking space in front of the animal hospital.

Bailey and Kate jumped out of the car and ran to the door. Mrs. Chang and Trina met them inside.

"The nurse is getting Biscuit," Kate said. "We already gave them our name."

Soon, the nurse came out with Biscuit on a leash. He limped on his bandaged paw, but when he saw Kate he hobbled on three legs to her, straining the leash.

"Hey, buddy!" Kate knelt so Biscuit could lick her face.

"I missed you!"

"Looks like he missed you, too!" the nurse said. "As you can see, we've bandaged his middle so his ribs will heal faster. Since the bandage only sticks to itself, you can remove it in a week or two. Just try to keep him as calm as possible for the next couple of weeks. No jumping up or down onto furniture."

"What about his paw?" Bailey asked. "Do we need to know anything about that?"

"We had to stitch it up. Remove the bandage tomorrow and see how it looks. If the wound isn't oozy or bleeding, you don't need to rebandage it. But if it is, go ahead and bandage it up for another day. I'll send an extra one home with you." The nurse handed the bandage to Kate. "Just wrap it with the gauze and tape it so it's secure."

"Thank you for taking such good care of Biscuit," Kate said.

"We were happy to do it," the nurse replied. "If you have any questions about caring for his injuries, give us a call."

"We will," Kate said.

Mrs. Chang went to the counter and paid the bill while the girls headed to the car with Biscuit.

"I can't believe all that's happened this week." Bailey petted Biscuit, who laid his head on Kate's arm as she held him. "Do we have some things to tell the Camp Club Girls tonight!"

CHAPTER 12

Solutions

Back at the hotel, Kate made Biscuit a little bed of blankets on the floor and gently laid him on it. "I'm so glad to have you back, Biscuit," she cooed as she stroked his head. "You be a good boy and stay here while Bailey and I call the girls. We won't be long."

"Mom, Kate and I are going to sit in the lobby to call the Camp Club Girls."

"Okay," Mrs. Chang said and waved them out.

Bailey pulled her phone from her pocket and conferenced everyone in. "We've had quite a day," she told them.

"What's going on?" Sydney asked.

"Oh, nothing," Kate answered casually. "We came up with a solution to the elk mystery we've been working on all week."

Four girls screamed, and Bailey held the phone away from her ear and laughed.

"How'd you do it?" McKenzie asked.

"Actually, we figured it out earlier, but we still had to

prove we were right," Bailey said.

Kate laughed and jumped into storytelling mode. "We went to the hospital to see Justin and Joe's grandpa. Just after we got to his room, the boys went into the hall."

"We decided to follow them to make sure they were okay," Bailey said. "You know, in case they were upset by seeing their grandpa or something."

"We found them in the hall," Kate said. "We overheard Joe telling Justin that they had to tell what happened."

"We didn't know what to do at first." Bailey took up the story. "But pretty soon we asked if we could do something to help."

"We got them to tell us what the problem was." Kate looked at Bailey.

"So? What was it?" Alex asked.

"Justin admitted he'd been shooting at the elk to scare them into stampeding," Bailey blabbed.

"No way! Oscar the Grouch confessed?" Alex screeched.

"You were right all along!" Elizabeth said.

"I feel bad about calling him Oscar now," Bailey said. "He's really not so bad after you get to know him."

"What about his brother?" McKenzie asked.

"Joe tried to talk Justin out of doing it, and went with him," Kate said. "So he was involved, but not really."

"Except by association," Elizabeth said. "Proverbs says a person is known by the company he or she keeps."

"Yeah, but when it's your brother, it's hard to stay away

from him." Bailey felt sorry Joe had gotten mixed up in his brother's mess.

"I wonder how they knew where to find the elk," Sydney said.

"Remember the smelly wallow we told you about that we found on our hike?" Bailey pulled her lip balm from her pocket and put some on. "We realized the boys must be using them to find the elk."

"But here's the good part," Kate said. "We encouraged Justin to tell his parents and told him we'd even go with him. He was afraid to. But then I told him God would give him the strength."

"So did he do it?" Sydney asked.

"Yep," Kate replied. "He walked right in there and told them everything."

"How'd they take it?" Alex asked.

"Pretty well, considering," Bailey said. "But they'll both have some kind of consequences."

"Guess that's to be expected," Elizabeth said.

"Wow," Sydney said. "You guys *have* had quite a day."

Bailey shifted her phone to the other ear. "We got Biscuit back."

"Already?" McKenzie asked. "How is he?"

"He's bandaged to keep him from moving too much," Kate answered. "That will give his ribs a chance to heal. We're supposed to keep him quiet. We can take the bandage off in a week."

"What about his foot?" Sydney asked.

"It's still wrapped up," Kate replied. "But we're supposed to look at it tomorrow to see if we can leave the bandage off."

"Wow, God really answered our prayers that he would heal fast," Elizabeth said. "I'm still surprised he wasn't killed in that stampede. God sure watched out for him."

Kate inhaled deeply. "I've thought the same thing. It's a relief to have him back home. I must have told God thank You a bazillion times already!"

The girls laughed.

"Now we'll just pray that God keeps working on Justin and Joe," Elizabeth said.

"Funny how we were so afraid of them before and now we're hoping they'll come to talk," Bailey said. "God sure turns things upside down."

"I've got to go," Sydney said. "But keep me posted."

"We should get going, too," Bailey said. "We'll let you know if anything more happens."

Bailey and Kate went back into their hotel room. Biscuit slept on the little bed Kate made him on the floor and hadn't moved at all. He lifted his shaggy head when they came through the door.

Mrs. Chang was lost in a book and Trina was looking out the window. "Hey, the Perkinses are coming back from the hospital," she said.

Bailey and Kate went to the window and saw the family walk up to the main entrance.

"Hey, maybe we can introduce Justin and Joe to the ghost in the Music Room tomorrow," Kate said.

"Mom, can we go ask when they get up here?"

"I think that would be a nice gesture," Mrs. Perkins said, "just so they don't wonder if we think less of them after what happened."

Bailey and Kate waited until they heard the Perkinses' voices in the hall before going out to greet them.

"We were wondering if Justin and Joe would like to come to the Music Room with us tomorrow," Bailey said. "There's a ghost who lives there!"

The Perkins family laughed.

"That would be fun, but we can't," Justin said. Then he looked at his parents and gave a sheepish grin. "We're pretty much grounded for the rest of our lives."

"Ohhh," Kate said. "We hadn't thought about that. Sorry."

"It's okay." Joe elbowed his older brother. "He's grounded longer than I am. Maybe if you come back again next year about this time I'll be free to go with you. But Justin probably can't for a few more years."

Justin playfully punched Joe in the arm.

"But we told our parents that you talked to us about your faith," Justin said. "They said we could have you over to talk to us again if you wouldn't mind."

"Mind?" Bailey said, her eyes growing to the size of tennis balls. "We'd love to!"

"So that pretty much covers it," Bailey told the Camp Club Girls. "We're going over to talk to them tomorrow afternoon, and our parents might even come, too."

"That is so cool," Elizabeth said. "You really let your light shine. Knowing Jesus and living a life of faith will be the best solution for their lives."

"For sure," Kate agreed. "And thanks to all of us working together, we have a solution to our mysteries."

Bailey giggled. "I can't wait to see what our next one will be!"

Join the Camp Club Girls online!

www.campclubgirls.com

❁ Get to know your favorite
Camp Club Girl in the
Featured Character section.

❊ Print your own bookmarks to use
in your favorite Camp Club Book!

❊ Get the scoop on upcoming adventures!

(Make sure to ask your mom and dad first!)

FOLLOW THE CAMP CLUB GIRLS

Book 1:
Mystery at Discovery Lake
ISBN 978-1-60260-267-0

Book 2:
Sydney's DC Discovery
ISBN 978-1-60260-268-7

Book 3:
McKenzie's Montana Mystery
ISBN 978-1-60260-269-4

Book 4:
Alexis and the
Sacramento Surprise
ISBN 978-1-60260-270-0

Book 5:
Kate's Philadelphia Frenzy
ISBN 978-1-60260-271-7

Book 6:
Bailey's Peoria Problem
ISBN 978-1-60260-272-4

IN ALL THEIR ADVENTURES!

Book 7:
Elizabeth's Amarillo Adventure
ISBN 978-1-60260-290-8

Book 10:
Kate's Vermont Venture
ISBN 978-1-60260-293-9

Book 8:
Sydney's Outer Banks Blast
ISBN 978-1-60260-291-5

Book 11:
McKenzie's Oregon Operation
ISBN 978-1-60260-294-6

Book 9:
Alexis and the Arizona Escapade
ISBN 978-1-60260-292-2

Available wherever books are sold.